The Other End of the Corridor

The Other End of the Corridor

Sujata Rajpal

MAHAVEER PUBLISHERS

Published by
MAHAVEER PUBLISHERS
4675A-21, Second Floor, Ansari Road,
Daryaganj, New Delhi – 110002
Ph. : 011 – 66629669–89, 23244999
e-mail : mahaveerpublishers@gmail.com
website : www.mahaveerpublishers.com

First Edition : January 2015

The Other End of the Corridor
ISBN (10) : 9350881012
ISBN (13): 9789350881019

This novel is entirely a work of fiction. Names, characters and incidents portrayed in it are the work of the author's imagination. Any resemblance to actual persons, living or dead, events or localities is entirely coincidental.

Distributed in India by
VAIBHAV BOOK SERVICE
e-mail : vaibhavbookservice@gmail.com

Distributed in Nepal by
BAJRANGBALI BOOK ENTERPRISES PVT. LTD.
Jyatha Mushyabahal, Ward No. 27, Kathmandu, Nepal
e-mail : bajrangbalibooks@gmail.com

Printed in India

For my Parents

Sharda and Yash Gulati

ACKNOWLEDGEMENTS

Adversity has the effect of eliciting talents which, in prosperous circumstances, would have lain dormant

– Horace

The Other End of the Corridor would have never happened but for that dynamic journalist who called me ignorant, and my ex-boss who made me feel useless. I thank both of them for sowing the seed in me to do something worthwhile.

My parents were my first readers. Thanks for inculcating in me the discipline to write each day no matter what. Their encouraging words to be perseverant kept me going.

I would always be indebted to Ms Urvashi Butalia of Zubaan for giving me her valuable feedback, which helped me flesh out the story and narrate it exactly the way I wanted to.

Writing is considered a lonely drive but to become a published author one needs an army of readers, critics, editors and well-wishers. This book wouldn't be what it is, were it not for –

My elder sister - Anita Soni for reading the manuscript and for making immense contribution to take this project to conclusion. My younger sister – Jyotsna Khera for her insightful help with the plot. Thank you for making my life more meaningful.

My Editors – Rasana Atreya, Harsh Agarwal and Namrata. Interestingly, I have never met Namrata in person but she was just a WhatsApp message away to handhold me at every stage of this book. Namrata, I can never thank you enough!

Deepika Rao, Annapurna and Karthik Nag – for patiently listening to new story ideas and reading the manuscript.

Sharanya Rao and Shirley Iyaz for fixing the grammar.

Mom, Dad, and my aunt Kusam Gulati for the most strenuous job of proofreading.

Ravi Sethi, Sudhir Kant, Sanjay Arora, Nethra Anjanappa and my Toastmasters fraternity who made the journey smooth in countless ways.

SPI, the wonderful organization that I work for, helped me discover my true passion.

Binay Dutta, PK Das and the entire team of Mahaveer Publishers – it was a pleasure working with you.

Ink Studioz for the brilliant cover design.

My 'suns' - Nikhil and Rahul who are my biggest critics and ardent fans.

Rajiv - for putting up with my mood swings, whims and my endless hours in front of the computer. Every happiness of my life would have been incomplete without you.

And God, for His blessings in various forms.

CHAPTER 1

I open my eyes. I can't see anything. Either I have gone blind or it's just pitch dark everywhere. I feel I have been hit by something on my head. It is hurting badly. I want to run away from here but I can barely stand. I am feeling dizzy. I wave my hands around in an aimless way. I can only feel the walls. It is claustrophobic. I am scared. I touch the walls again. I realize, it's a corridor... a dark corridor. I am confused. Should I step forward? But what about the monsters that this darkness veils! What about the traps that have been set! But, I shall move. I shall survive. I shall reach the other end of the corridor.

My Patiala salwar swished in the air as I stepped in the room wearing a pale blue, cotton salwar kameez; my waist length hair tied in a tight plait. After greeting the guests in a polite namaste, I sat next to my mother on a red plastic chair in our lower middle class drawing room in Patiala, a small town in Punjab. My mother's brow wrinkled when she saw me in old faded clothes, and not the bright magenta salwar kameez set especially stitched for such occasions.

"Leela is an excellent cook; *besan ke ladoo* is her specialty. She couldn't cook anything today because she had gone to college," Mummy said in a fabricated tone. I was being sold.

I frowned in disgust; I didn't even know the ingredients of the *ladoo*!

I felt like a piece of furniture in the market. The prospective customers came; sometimes they didn't like the colour, sometimes the design was faulty, and sometimes it just didn't appeal to them. The rejections didn't bother me. I was probably just a manufacturing defect, I giggled to myself. The entire world seemed to be obsessed with milky white skin and extra slim women.

What was I doing here? I asked myself. A bubbly, broad-minded girl of nineteen should be in college studying or having fun with her friends, and not sitting in front of probable suitors. I lifted my chin up and gazed at my father sitting opposite me, on a *diwan* next to the boy's father. With a deadpan expression, Daddy ji slurped tea from the borrowed bone china cup, making a sucking sound each time the cup touched his lips. Every time a suitor came to see me, Mummy would borrow a bone china tea set from the neighbours to serve tea to the boy's family. I looked at my father, his cold composure sending shivers down my bones. Daddy ji's eyes were fixed on the deep red embroidered tablecloth covering our fourteen-inch black and white television set. I couldn't hide my fear or run away from the fact that my father could do anything he wanted; even if it meant marrying me off to some old, lecherous man or a dead corpse. No one would say a word. My mother didn't have a voice of her own and even if she did, she never opened her mouth in his presence. Otherwise a cheerful, talkative woman, she bowed down to the dictates of my father - the self-proclaimed emperor of the house.

Daddy ji, home, and my elder brother Sanjay were the nucleus of Mummy's life. I was last in her list of priorities. My parents never argued, never fought because my father ordered, and we all obeyed. My mother was a woman of the nineteenth century, she believed whatever her husband did, was for the good of her. Sometimes I wondered whether she ever thought of herself as a separate entity. I didn't want to live a life like my mother's, mutely suffering a husband's dictates.

I knew that like the others, this one, too, would reject me. My dark complexion, ordinary looks, our dingy two-bedroom house, my father's cycle with a loud bell on which he commuted to work; there was nothing remarkable about me that could lure potential buyers.

Leela, my name, was my first stumbling block; it made me feel like an old spinster, and not a girl of nineteen. I grew up hating my name. When I was born, I was named Leelavati, after my great grandmother, but my parents decided to do away with the suffix 'vati' in my class ten certificate. And as if all this was not enough, I was a *manglik*, which meant I had flaws in my horoscope, making it hard to find a suitable boy for me. According to Pandit ji, a *manglik* girl could marry only a *manglik* boy.

Haunted by the thoughts of an unmarried daughter, Daddy ji started his search for a groom early, believing it would take him five to six years to find a match - the way it had taken for Mummy's sister. In the last six months, Pandit ji had brought three proposals: one was twenty years my senior, the other was a widower with a two-year-old baby. Another proposal that had come a month ago was almost finalized, but the boy's family backed out after saying yes.

Despite all the negatives in my life, my one asset gave me hope - my distinctive voice. Warm and friendly, it is exactly the kind of voice radio announcers have and I was proud of it. All my classmates and even the senior girls of our college used to say, I have a smiling voice; that is when I speak, it sounds as if I am smiling. I had always wanted to be a Radio Jockey for as long as I can remember.

Once, an RJ from a radio station in Chandigarh came to Patiala to record a live show. People thronged from even the neighbouring towns to hear her live. The stadium was crowded, with people jostling and shoving each other to get a glimpse of the RJ. The people were expecting to see a woman who would have a beautiful face like her voice but she was just the opposite. She was short, and had honey coloured skin. In spite of not being a 'svelte beauty', she had an aura about her. The realization that the entire stadium was waiting on the words of that one woman gave me a heady feeling. It was thrilling to experience the power of one person's popularity on unknown people. That RJ remained the talking point for the people of our town for months after the show. I was ten years old then and didn't know about the Radio Jockeys, but I decided that day that I wanted to be famous. I didn't know what it would take to become an RJ, I didn't know what qualifications I would need to acquire to get there, I only knew that RJs spoke nonstop and had to be knowledgeable about music. I was already very talkative; I just needed to learn about music! From then on, my tiny black transistor radio, playing the latest songs from Hindi movies, was my constant companion. But how the hell was I going to ward off the dark clouds of marriage hovering over me?

"Come, sit here." Breaking my reverie, the boy's mother called out to me, pointing to the chair next to her.

Vishal, the boy in question, was thirty years old, 5' 11", heavily built, and didn't look that bad. He was an engineer, and worked as a senior executive for a pharmaceutical firm in Delhi. His mother was the headmistress of a school in Delhi, and his father, a professor in Aligarh. His younger sister was married and lived in the US. Vishal was a seemingly perfect match – tall, fair, the only son, from an educated family who owned a house and a motor bike. The fact that a high profile family like theirs had agreed to come to our house to see me had lifted me in the eyes of my parents.

"Vishal is planning to start his own business," his mother announced proudly.

His father nodded in affirmation as the mother spoke smugly about their son's achievements. I kept my gaze down, focusing on the plate of *ladoos* on the table; they all were of different shapes, some were round – the perfect shape, some egg shaped, some tiny and some big. Vishal looked everywhere, but not at me. He didn't ask me anything except how I did in my exams.

"Fine," I replied and kept my eyes downcast, fixed on the plate. Only one, the most imperfect shaped, was left on the plate now.

Like me, Vishal was a *manglik*, and according to Pandit ji, our horoscopes matched perfectly. Vishal's parents had been looking for a bride for their son for many years. Initially they rejected girls who were *manglik*, but didn't fit into the description of a perfect bride. With every passing year, their patience and hope waned.

"Her stars are very lucky for her spouse's career and health," Pandit ji said, reading from my horoscope. "He will reach the zenith of success. With her stars, he will make a name and fame for himself, go abroad in his thirties, and have his own flourishing business. She will also be very lucky for his family and will have good relations with her in-laws." Pandit ji looked up at the visitors, then back at the horoscope. "It's one in ten million cases that all characteristics match one hundred per cent," he said earnestly.

This was the same Pandit ji who had condemned me as an inauspicious child when I was born. "Wherever she goes, she will bring misery and doom to those around her," he had declared ominously. Pandit ji's prophecy came true when my younger brother died of pneumonia at the age of one. The loss of a child shocked my mother, sending her into a shell. She recovered after many years. After the death of my little brother, my parents stopped loving me; my father remained furious all the time.

My parents never admitted this openly, but the thought that I was unwanted and unloved was etched in my mind. My desires always took a back seat in comparison to Sanjay's quirky demands. Wheatish complexion, light brown eyes, long eyelashes, black hair, Sanjay looked exactly like my mother. My father too was a handsome man. I was the only odd one out in the family.

"Your daughter looks so different," people would say. By different they meant, dark, ugly and unattractive. My brother was four years older than me but fought with me for every little thing; and my parents always supported him. This preferential treatment at home had sown the seeds of sibling rivalry between Sanjay and me.

I craved to hear words of appreciation from my parents, but they were so absorbed in pampering their son that they sometimes forgot that they had a daughter growing up in the house as well.

The only time I was ever given special care was when I fell sick. The 'special care' would mean food served to me in bed and a glass of milk at bedtime. How I wished I would get sick more often!

"Leela is ours now; we will talk to our Pandit ji and fix an auspicious date for the marriage," Vishal's mother said, putting a crisp five hundred rupee note in my palm. She dished out a one-rupee coin from her clutch purse and placed it on top of the note. She then shoved a small piece of *burfi* in my mouth.

Mummy and Daddy ji stood there with their mouths open; they could not believe their luck; their search for a *manglik* boy had ended sooner than expected and with a prize catch like Vishal to boot!

"What about my studies? I have yet to complete my graduation," I said. I was startled at the sudden turn of events. I had expected this boy-see-girl drama to continue for a few more years.

"You can appear for your exams privately," Daddy ji said stroking my hair lovingly. "And why are you so bothered about your studies? You don't need to work after marriage; Vishal is earning a very good salary."

This was one of those rare occasions when my father showered love on me.

"The boy is very tall, very good natured and his mother is so polite... very cultured family. Our daughter is very lucky; I knew she would get a good boy," Daddy ji rattled to whoever cared to listen.

I closed my eyes wearily. A shadow crossed over my face. How could I get married at nineteen?

But you wanted an escape and you are getting one, my inner voice told me. I feared that if I didn't agree to this alliance, my parents would tie me to whoever else was willing to marry me. Then my dream of becoming an RJ would remain just that - a dream. I told myself that Vishal was an educated man, unlike the good-for-nothing loafers of Patiala. Any girl with a background like mine would jump at such an opportunity, instead of deliberating over it. This alliance would provide me an opportunity to make a life outside a small town.

I daydream:

Vishal drops me off at the radio station early in the morning. I am dressed in a T- shirt and jeans, just like any other girl in a big city. My schedule is very hectic but I love it. My show is the most popular one on the radio. 'Good Morning, Delhi,' I begin the show in my cheerful voice. My mother-in-law tells everyone, 'You know, this is my daughter-in-law speaking!'

My wedding was the most talked about affair in Patiala. The entire circuit house was booked for the groom's party. Huge loans, caterers from the city, an expensive trousseau... everything had to match the status of the groom's family.

The narrow bylanes of our town were the star attraction for Vishal's NRI sister, Kiran, and her husband Navin.

I cried because all girls are supposed to cry when they get married and leave their parents' house but my tears dried as soon as the yellow and black cab carrying me to my marital home started moving, leaving my family behind. With dreams of a new life in the City of Opportunities, I closed my eyes as I sat beside my 'engineer husband' in the back seat, his mother occupying the front seat next to the driver. No one really bothered about his father; he was probably with the rest of the relatives in the bus. Noticing me doze off, Vishal rested my head gently on his shoulder with a brush of his hand. This was the first time I had come in close physical contact with a man who was not a relative. His body odour mingled with the lingering, strong scent of his cologne and the fragrance of roses in the car. I immersed myself in the smell of the man who had come into my life as a Messiah to uplift me from a nondescript life to a meaningful one in the capital of the country.

Life, here I come.

CHAPTER 2

It was a good four– and - a - half hour drive to Delhi. The cab carrying us came to a halt in the narrow driveway of my in-laws' spacious house in Rajouri Garden. The entire house was lit up with green and red twinkling lights. Celebrations to welcome the only daughter-in-law of the Chopra family were in full swing.

Vishal's mother, who was Ma to everyone irrespective of age and relation, was the first one to alight from the car. With a wave of her hand, she signalled the newlyweds to stay inside the car until a bottle of mustard oil was poured on both sides of the door, just before my grand entry into the house.

"Now you can come out," ordered Ma. "Right foot first."

Vishal stepped out first and walked over to stand next to his mother. I stuck my right foot out, but pulled it inside with a snap when I saw a huge, ferocious dog circling the car. I felt my face go pale despite the layers of foundation on it.

With a plate for *puja* in her hand, Ma waited impatiently for me to take my first step into the house. Vishal stood there with hands in his pockets and a bored look on his face.

"Come out quickly! The auspicious time to enter the house is ticking away. Don't be scared, Julie will not do anything to you!" someone screamed.

I looked at Vishal. Was he mocking my fear of dogs? I was dead scared of dogs. Small Pomeranians were alright, but a huge German Shepherd - Oh my God! How could Daddy ji have omitted this detail, when he was able to talk at length about the dimensions of their drawing room, the colour of their sofa, and the tall, black, iron gate that was a little rusted in the centre?

There was no greenery anywhere, except for a few potted plants kept near the entrance. By now Vishal had begun walking towards the door. He stopped when Ma instructed him to wait for me and walk by my side. Vishal had a confused look on his face. I had no clue what was going on in his mind at that moment. Was he judging me because I was acting like a scared child? Of course, not, how could he? Vishal was too mature a person to frame such a biased opinion of me.

"Come out, Leela Bhabhi!" Kiran extended her hand towards me, even as she made a futile attempt to conceal her grin.

Finally, I came out of the car. Julie sniffed at me, perhaps to make sure that I was the right choice for her master. Balancing an earthen pot filled with grains of rice on my head, I entered my in-laws' house. My house. My eyes still followed Julie cautiously, who kept appearing and disappearing from the scene.

I was made to sit down on stark white sheets. And there was I. Leela in red dress, on white sheets, with black hair, and brown *Mehandi* on hands. I smelt of Jasmine. It was beautiful. I was beautiful. For the first time I felt important. Children jostled each other to stand close to me. All eyes were fixed on me.

I heaved a sigh of relief when a child put a leash on Julie and took the dog outside. Despite the chaos of children jumping on the mattresses, there was a kind of discipline and order in the room. No one interrupted Ma when she said something.

Innumerable aunts and cousins posed in front of the camera as they thrust *ladoos* into my mouth.

While eating the *ladoos* I stole a glance or two at the drawing room. I noticed it was huge - almost as big as our entire house. Beige curtains were drawn on two tall windows. Three white sofas were pushed against the wall to make space for mattresses, the impromptu sleeping arrangements for a house full of relatives. An expensive oil painting depicting a village scene adorned the wall behind the sofa.

I thought of my parents' drawing room, where floral bed sheets passed for curtains. There were four plastic chairs, one sofa in cheap cane, an old plastic centre table, and a *diwan*. It would be fun telling this to Pushpa di who lived next door with her husband and two young sons. She was closer to Mummy in age, but she was more of my friend than my mother's. Pushpa di was the only person with whom I could share everything, well, almost everything.

The ceremonies had drained me. I wanted to just throw my badly crushed silk salwar kameez away and take off my shiny stilettos. I had never worn such high heels before, but if I was to match my 5' 3" height to Vishal's 5' 11" frame, I figured that I had better get used to it. I was escorted to a room upstairs and made to sit on a bedecked bed.

"Do not move from here till Bhaiya comes," ordered Kiran winking at me before gently closing the door behind her. I was too nervous to smile back at her.

I sat on the massive bed with my knees folded in front, my dupatta drawn over my head and face in a *ghunghat.* My arms adorned with two dozen red and cream ivory bangles rested delicately on my knees.

Two wooden cupboards on one side of the bed, a large study table, a rocking chair and a closed ventilator near the ceiling; my eyes scrutinized the room from under the dupatta that covered half of my face. Everything was arranged very neatly. A beautiful black and white portrait of Ma in her youth adorned the wall behind the bed.

My eyes searched for a water jug or bottle, but there wasn't any. I thought about the scenes of a couple's first night from the innumerable Hindi movies that I had watched with Pushpa di in Alka talkies. She had given me tips for the first night, but I seemed to be forgetting everything. I blushed, thinking of Vishal's arms around me.

Was I expected to be coy, like a small town girl, or reciprocate his aggression in bed?

My back ached from sitting stiffly in the same posture for quite some time. I was in half a mind to take off my heavy dupatta and lie down on the bed.

'Do not move till Bhaiya comes.' I was reminded of Kiran's instructions. Hearing the sound of soft footsteps, I straightened my stiff back and waited for my husband to relieve me from my backbreaking posture.

"You haven't changed yet; do you want to sleep in this fancy dress?" These were his first words.

Embarrassed, I quietly got down from the bed, the *ghunghat* still drawn over my face, and headed towards the bathroom to change. Pushpa di had forced me to buy a transparent nightgown in magenta for my 'wedding night', but I decided to wear a simple cotton one in a yellow floral print – something that didn't look fancy.

When I came out, Vishal had already changed and was sitting on the bed in an upright position, making it obvious that I had taken much longer than expected. Covering my bare shoulders with a towel, I made my way towards the bed and sat on its edge.

"It's very hot," I said. Talking about the weather seemed like a safer way to start a conversation.

"Do you think so? It's rather cold at this hour." Vishal gave me a look that made me feel like an idiot.

Am I so stupid that I don't even know the difference between hot and cold? I bit my lower lip.

An eerie silence spread across the room. After a few minutes, which seemed like eternity, Vishal's arm reached out for me in a quick embrace, the soft tinkling of my bangles breaking the silence. With his other hand, he switched off the light, and switched on the zero watt bulb. He buried his head in my chest and murmured something inaudible. I dug my fingers in his hair when his body enveloped mine. I let out a soft moan when his mouth searched for my nipples. Light from the staircase pierced through the cracks in the closed ventilator near the ceiling. I could see the back of my husband's dark head in the diffused light from the night bulb. I didn't know what was expected of me; I simply allowed my husband to direct me. I closed my eyes tightly as his hips roughly pumped into me.

Even before I could feel my body respond to his touch, I found myself lying next to him, his body drenched in perspiration, my eyes staring at the three still blades of the ceiling fan above us. Julie barked outside as if she saw my virginity walking out of the door. It was over. Without a word, without sweet nothings whispered in my ears, under the gloomy dim yellow light, the act was accomplished for me as well as for my brand new husband.

Damn it, this wasn't how Pushpa di had told me. I couldn't remember whether my husband's hair was straight like mine or curly. Whether it was brownish, or black; whether the sides of his thin black moustache reached his lower lip or stopped at the corner of his upper lip. Did his gums show when he smiled?

A glass of water to cool my parched throat was the only thing I could think of. I felt my throat choking with thirst. I looked at Vishal; he was asleep, his back turned to me, brown checked blanket pulled over him. Only a part of his head was visible. Through the blur of floating emotions, I stared intensely at the visible part of his head; the person sleeping next to me was still a stranger. I hadn't met him alone even once. I knew nothing about him except his official bio data. My parents had allowed a complete stranger to sleep with their daughter. Tears filled my eyes. I didn't know whether my tears were because of some hormonal thing, or whether I was missing home, but they just flowed, and I let them.

Arranged marriages are like this; you can't help but tie yourself to a person you know nothing about, I thought, trying to console myself. I told myself that most marriages in India are arranged and most of them are successful, just like mine would be.

CHAPTER 3

I was woken up by the sound of water gushing out from the shower in the bathroom. The pillow next to mine was kept at its place, the blanket folded neatly. The bed sheet on Vishal's side of the bed had been straightened. I tried to go back to sleep, but the noise of continuous chatting outside didn't allow me to. Filtered rays of the sun streamed into the room through the window, which opened into the rear side of the house. I lay still on the bed with my eyes wide open, the blanket pulled to my chin, thinking of the days leading up to my marriage.

My thoughts went back to the day I had gone to our neighbour Sumitra aunty's house to return the silver tray that Mummy had borrowed for the ring ceremony. I overheard Sumitra aunty talking to her cleaning lady.

"He might not have found anybody because he is a *manglik*. That's probably why he agreed to marry Leela. There isn't any other match between them. Did you see how handsome he is?"

I pretended not to have heard her.

Let her say anything she wants, I told myself, I know everyone in Patiala is jealous of me.

"Congrats! I heard your fiancé is a manager in a big company," Sumitra aunty's son Ranbir said as I was about to leave.

"Yes, that's right! Vishal is a sales executive, his mother is a headmistress, and his sister lives in America, his father..."

"Enough enough... everyone in Patiala knows about it. But there is something which no one else knows," Ranbir said, jumping in front of me and grabbing me by the shoulders.

"Ranbir! Leave me, someone will see us." I freed myself from his grip and pushed him against the wall. "Get out of my way! You couldn't complete your education, you failed twice! I would be ashamed to even talk to my parents about you. I can never have any feelings for you, so stop... stop thinking about me and get married to someone who suits you," I hissed, sprinting out of their house before anyone could see me talking to him.

"Leela, you will never be happy without me," I heard Ranbir call out.

Ranbir was a few years senior to me in school. After two failed attempts in college, he dropped out and started assisting his father in their rice export business.

One day Pushpa di saw Ranbir following me to the college. She asked me if I too was interested in him.

"We are different in every way possible. He is an uneducated fellow, and I have big dreams of becoming a Radio Jockey. He is just like all the other boys in Patiala-conservative and backward. How could he possibly understand my aspirations? I could never be happy marrying a hooligan like him," I told Pushpa di.

I didn't like Ranbir at all. His short and stout posture, uncouth behaviour and ungraceful manners were repulsive. I balked at the thought of even befriending him.

"Leela, you are still sleeping?" Ma came out from the bathroom, her hair wrapped in a thin orange towel. I was startled by Ma's sudden presence in front of me. It was my mother-in-law and not Vishal in the bathroom. I gathered myself and quickly got down from the bed to touch Ma's feet as an Indian gesture of greeting elders.

"Get ready quickly; all the relatives are waiting for you downstairs," Ma instructed, lightly touching my head in response to my gesture.

"Where is he?" I somehow gathered courage to ask about my husband. I didn't want to say my husband's name in front of my mother-in-law. I had never heard Mummy say Daddy ji's name aloud.

"Where is Daddy ji?" she would ask us.

"He has gone out for an urgent work and will be back in some time," Ma replied as she dashed out of the room, giving me a curt look conveying that I didn't need to know more.

I hurried to the bathroom and secured the latch on the top as well as bottom. I turned the shower on and let the cold water run over my body. When I came out after the shower, I noticed an off-white sari on the bed probably left by Ma while I was having bath. It was a lovely sari in expensive tissue, with intricate Zardosi work in gold all over.

Kiran entered my room, spreading a row of necklaces on the bed.

"Wear this *Kundan choker;* it will go very well with gold work on this sari." Without giving me any time to respond, Kiran started putting long danglers in my ears. My smile widened when I saw the glittering pieces of jewellery. I had never seen such expensive jewellery in real gold before. Mummy had one ten gram gold necklace, which she had kept safely in the bank locker, taking it out only to wear for the weddings of close relatives. For everyday use, she had one gold chain which she never removed from her neck, and a pair of small gold round earrings passed on to her by her grandmother.

The white sari and gold jewels complemented my honey coloured skin perfectly. Every visible part of my body was adorned with jewels. Two fat gold chains, one huge necklace, three rings, one dozen gold bangles, gold anklets; I looked like a mannequin in the showcase of Khanna Jewellers. I loved the smell of gold.

Was this really me? I admired my image in the full-length mirror in the room.

When I came out of my room, Ma introduced me to the women from the neighbourhood who had come to see the new bride. I smiled coyly when they admired my clothes and jewels. I felt blessed. Wealth had never been a priority for me when I thought of a husband. If it ever was, I would have readily accepted Ranbir's proposal. I wanted an educated and progressive thinking man, but now, it seemed that God had blessed me with everything that a woman could ask for.

It was only later that I learnt from one of Vishal's aunts that except for one gold chain and four bangles, all the other jewellery given to me was artificial. Of course, I was disappointed, but more than that, I felt cheated. My in-laws belonged to the middle class and I didn't expect them to load me with gold and diamonds, but when ordinary stones were presented to me in shiny velvet boxes with fake gold seals to make them look like real, it amounted to sheer fraud in my mind. However, I let it pass and gracefully accepted what was given to me. I didn't feel the need to discuss it with my parents; I didn't want to ruin their happiness.

CHAPTER 4

Ma was the headmistress of a high school. 'Mrs. Shobha Chopra, B.Ed, M.Ed Mathematics (Honours)', her name shone on the brass nameplate nailed to the iron gate outside. 'Prof. Manohar Lal Chopra', the name of Vishal's father was mentioned above her name in a smaller font. Ma was always smartly dressed; a neatly pinned printed silk or cotton sari, two slim gold bangles on one wrist, a watch on the other, thin gold chain, understated lip colour, big round red bindi between her brows, thin gold framed spectacles resting on her nose and neatly combed henna dyed hair held back tightly in a bun. Even in her fifties Ma was very agile; she could multitask with ease and perfection. With water kept on the stove for tea, she would chop vegetables for lunch. In between sips of sugary, milky tea, she rolled *paranthas* and filled the water jugs with drinking water. With the agility of a person in her twenties, she shuttled between the kitchen, various rooms and veranda, yelling instructions to everyone. Her influence permeated the house.

There were rules for everything in the house. The meals were served at a fixed time and only on the dining table. It was not like meals in our house. Back at home, Mummy would eat only after cleaning the kitchen, and I would eat alone on the terrace, long after everyone had gone to sleep, my small transistor playing the latest Hindi songs.

I marvelled at Ma's poise and efficiency, but soon this awe turned into irritability when I realized I was expected to toe the line. Household work didn't interest me. Though I did help Ma in the kitchen sometimes, expecting me to become a perfectionist like her was a little too much.

I loved my three cups of tea, sipped one after the other; true, it was one cup water, a pinch of tea powder, a dash of grated ginger and a few drops of lemon. It was odd, but it was the kind of tea I liked.

"No one drinks tea immediately after lunch in my house, make tea in the evening," Ma instructed, switching off the gas when she saw me making tea after lunch.

The cabinets remained locked all the time. A tiny lock hung on the phone, and its key dangled along with the other keys on a silver key chain hooked onto Ma's sari, making a tinkling sound whenever she moved.

For Ma, her house was like her school and its inhabitants like unruly schoolchildren who always needed a whip to discipline them. Vishal was her favourite student, who rarely did anything wrong. Vishal's photographs, in innumerable poses, adorned the walls of the house. Every milestone of his life... his first step as one year old, the first day at school, fifth birthday, almost everything had pictorial representation. Ma loved to narrate incidents from her son's childhood. When home at the same time, mother and the son were inseparable.

Vishal would get panicky if he did not see Ma around. "Where… where… has Ma gone? She isn't in the kitchen!"

"Where will Ma go? She must be on the terrace, or in her room." I would get irritated when he behaved like a small pup, feeling lost without his mother.

My father-in-law, whom Vishal addressed as Papa, was a professor of Biochemistry at Aligarh Muslim University. He lived in a rented single bedroom house in Aligarh, visiting Delhi once every three months for a few days.

I had heard the saga of Ma's professional struggle and her sacrifice for her children many times from Vishal. How Papa had to stay in Aligarh and Ma had to move to Delhi so that Vishal and Kiran could have better education. Other than Vishal extolling the virtues of his mother, there was not much verbal interaction between us.

Ma resumed her work two weeks after the wedding. She left for school in the morning and returned only at four. Vishal was still on leave. An impending sales conference had nipped our honeymoon plans in the bud. Though our time alone could have compensated for the missed honeymoon, the atmosphere at home was far from romantic. I expected my marriage to be like what I watched in films; the hero wooing the heroine with roses, a hurried kiss at the door, clandestine holding of hands under the table, make-up sex after a fight... Real life, however, didn't have even a hint of the reel world. Vishal was always either on the phone or on his computer. The moment I approached him with a loving romantic gesture, his stiff body language, and the cold look in his eyes, would take the romance out of me.

"How many days leave have you taken?" I asked Vishal curiously, when he didn't go to the office even after a month. It was unusual for me to see a man sitting at home doing nothing but smoke. I still hadn't adjusted to the conspicuous odour of smoke in the house.

"I lost my job a few months ago," he replied candidly. The truth had to erupt one day; how long could he pretend to be working from home after all? He didn't meet my eyes when he spoke.

"Our company was acquired by a European company and many employees were asked to leave. The company gave me a good retrenchment compensation," he told me with moist eyes.

I saw a deep depression in his eyes. I felt sorry for him. It could be frustrating for a man to lose his job.

"No problem, look for another one," I said, trying to lift up his spirits.

It was only later I learnt from one of the relatives that the fake gold jewellery was only the tip of the iceberg. Vishal just had a B.Sc degree from a third rate college, and was not an Engineer and an MBA as his parents had so proudly claimed. Though he was very intelligent, he had never held a steady job. The acquisition was not the reason for the loss of his job; he was terminated by his company over disciplinary issues. I didn't see any prudence in confronting Vishal about it. I knew the truth behind it would never surface.

I was legally wedded to him. Divorcing him wasn't really an option and what was more, I didn't want to. I was still better off marrying an unemployed man from an educated family in Delhi, than living in the unloved, glum atmosphere of my parents' house, or even marrying an old widower who my parents had shortlisted.

This is your destiny now, I told myself. You better get used to it.

CHAPTER 5

"Vishal, do you know," I said, as I lay on the bed with my head on his lap, "I want to become an RJ; it's my dream."

Vishal was engrossed in reading a book, his fingers running through my hair as my head rested on his lap. I told him about the RJ I had met when I was ten years old, looking dreamily at the cover of his book above my face.

"Vishal!" I pushed the book away from my face when he didn't respond.

He said nothing. The book was back in its position, above my face.

"Vishal, do you know someone in any of the radio stations in Delhi? I want to find out more about being an RJ. If you don't have a job, at least I can work and help."

I waited for him to respond. Then I felt his fingers tugging at my hair.

"Ouch, it hurts," I whimpered.

He suddenly took a fistful of my hair and tugged it really hard. Before I could think further, he pounded the book on my face, his heavy blow catching me unawares. I cupped my nose, shrieking in pain.

"I am so sorry," he apologized when he saw blood oozing from my nose. Then he helped me wash off the blood in the bathroom.

"I got angry because you reminded me of the fact that I am unemployed," he explained. "I am very sorry."

I was shaken up by his bizarre behaviour. I thought it was happening to someone else or it was just a bad dream. My tears wouldn't stop thinking how my husband could treat me so violently over such a small thing. I remained in a state of shock for the next two days. Later, I convinced myself that I must pull myself together; I was sure Vishal was a gentleman and it was just a stray incident.

One night, Ma and Vishal had just sat down for dinner and I was still shuttling between the dining room and the kitchen to bring the last minute things on to the table.

"Ma!" I said, "Did Mummy call you about Sanjay's marriage on the twenty eighth of next month? Mummy wants me to come at least two weeks before the wedding; she wants my help with the preparations. She had called again this morning. You didn't even inform me that she had called," I asked, a smile playing on my lips constantly. I didn't want to sound rude even though I was angry at Ma for not conveying the message to me.

Ma continued eating her food without looking up.

"You, Papa and Vishal can come back after the wedding, but I will stay for a few more days. I haven't met my friends for a long time," I announced.

Ma was silent for a moment. She set down the morsel of food that she was about to eat, back on her plate. I was approaching the dining table with a jug in my hand. She got up from her chair and shoved me with unexpected force. I was startled by her reaction. I prevented myself from falling by grabbing the nearest chair.

"How dare you question me? How dare you? I am not your secretary; I do not need to inform you of everything that happens in this house. And who are you to plan things without asking me? Vishal doesn't even lift his finger without asking me. Even now, when he is thirty-one, he doesn't; and you? How dare you?" Ma yelled.

"Didn't inform me," Ma mimicked me. "Look how this girl talks!" She gave me a dirty look before dashing off to her room.

Vishal continued eating his food as if nothing had happened.

His indifference blew my lid off.

"How can you eat your food when your mother is hitting your wife?" I grabbed his shoulders and shook him roughly.

"She is not hitting you," he replied politely. "Go and say sorry to Ma. Look! Because of you, she has left her food unfinished." He caught hold of both my hands to stop me from shaking him. "You have hurt Ma. You should have asked her before planning your trip; and you even planned for all of us! Ma decides everything in this house. No one else, not even Papa."

I was aghast.

"What if I had fallen on the floor with a glass jug, what if the glass had pierced my feet?"

"Did anything happen?" he replied, giving me an accusing look. I was trembling with fear. He loosened his grip on my wrists when he saw tears in my eyes.

"Go and say sorry to Ma," he instructed once again.

I was scared to upset Vishal; my nose still hurt.

"I'm sorry Ma," I apologized.

Ultimately, after much persuasion, Ma came back to the table and finished her dinner, but it was still undecided whether I would go for the wedding or not. I was scared to bring this topic up again, but I had to. The date of the wedding was fast approaching. I decided to persuade Vishal to allow me to go, may be just for a day.

Vishal was sitting cross-legged on the bed reading the morning's paper when I entered the bedroom after cleaning the kitchen.

"Vishal," I mewed.

"Yes, tell me?" he asked keeping the newspaper aside. For once I had his undivided attention.

"You went to Patiala only four months ago, you can't go this month. Ma is receiving an award from the government on the twenty-eighth. It's a very big event; you have to attend the function. What will her staff say, the Headmistress is getting an award and her only daughter- in - law is not there? Even Papa is coming. Leela! You know how people talk in Delhi, it is not like your Patiala; we have a status, and we have to be bothered about it. Let's not talk about your going again."

"But Vishal, Sanjay is my only brother, and all the relatives will be there. Everyone will talk if I don't go."

"You are only bothered about what your relatives will say, you are not at all concerned about what Ma's staff, and our relatives will think, and most importantly, how Ma will feel. If you still want to go, then go, but there is no need for you to come back. You can stay there forever. You decide what you want to do." Vishal picked up the newspaper and started reading it again.

"Please Vishal, try to understand, I have to go, it's Sanjay's Wedding," I begged. It was disgusting. I had to plead to attend my brother's wedding. I had no freedom, no control over my life. I felt claustrophobic.

"Go, then, but only after my death." Saying this, he jumped out of the bed and sprinted off to the bathroom. He was out in seconds. A bottle of liquid toilet cleaner materialized in his hand as he stood in front of me.

Before I could make sense of his words and actions, he was holding the bottle to his mouth, the nozzle almost touching his lips.

"Do you want to go? After my funeral, you can go wherever you want."

I was too traumatized to react. My head was spinning at the thought of what might happen if he swallowed the acid or it fell into his eyes. Finally, I gathered myself and jumped with all my might to snatch the bottle from his hand, but this only encouraged him in his mission. He squeezed the bottle. In our struggle, a few drops fell on the floor, but thankfully, nothing fell on him. He didn't let go of the bottle.

I was stunned beyond words.

"Ma, see what Vishal is doing!" I wailed.

Ma didn't hear me; she was asleep.

I was scared out of my wits. I had heard of people losing all their senses in anger, taking their own lives, killing others in rage, but such things happened in stories and news reports, with people we didn't know.

I tugged at him and kept begging him to leave the bottle aside. I was not sure if he understood the consequences of his actions. He was angry with me. He was risking not just his life but mine too. The acid could harm both of us.

I begged, I threatened, I shouted, I cried, but he kept repeating, "I will die right now in front of your eyes, and then you go wherever you want to go."

I was fighting a losing battle. He was physically stronger than me; I couldn't have overpowered him. I resigned myself to my fate. I took my face in my hands and sobbed uncontrollably.

"I will not leave you and go anywhere, don't kill yourself, please don't kill yourself, I will do whatever you say," I promised in between sobs.

On the day of Sanjay's wedding, I desperately wished I could have been there with my parents. Not that it would have mattered to them emotionally, but they would have felt proud introducing their well-off daughter to their guests.

I expected Sanjay to request Vishal to allow me to go, but he didn't. Even though we had our jealousies and differences, I was his only sibling.

"Leela, it's okay if you can't make it for the wedding. Come some other time," he said coldly.

In spite of everything, I wanted to be with my parents on that happy occasion. I hoped against hope for a miracle. I kept praying, but my prayers were not answered.

On the twenty-eighth, the day Sanjay wore a *Sehra* and mounted the mare to go to his bride's house, the day my parents' house was lit up with twinkling lights to celebrate the marriage of their only son, the day their entire house was abuzz with dance and music, I sat in the front row of the state auditorium, along with my husband and father-in-law and, applauded for the students who excelled in academics and extracurricular activities. I also applauded for the teachers who were recognized for being the role models for their students. With a scornful smile playing on my lips, I clapped the loudest when my mother-in-law went on the stage to receive an award for being the most efficient administrator.

That night Vishal made love to me with gusto. After he was done, he told me that he was very proud of his mother. He also told me that I had made him happy by not attending my brother's wedding for his sake. That night, unlike the other nights when he would turn his face to the other side and go to sleep as soon as the act was done, he wanted to talk his heart out, his fingers running through my hair as he spoke.

I listened in silence. His bizarre behaviour the other day had scared me to death. He lectured me on becoming a role model for our yet-to-be-born children.

"A woman is held in high reverence when she sacrifices for the family," he went on. "I want you to become proficient in household work, and methodical like Ma," he said, caressing my cheeks lovingly.

The route to a man's heart is through his mother's; I understood my first lesson for a happy marriage that day. I could not become perfect like Ma, but I decided to take more interest in household chores for the happiness of my husband. That was the only way I could secure my place in the family.

Vishal is not a bad person; he is stressed because of his job. After getting a job, he will become loving and caring, I told myself.

CHAPTER 6

My sister-in-law, Kiran was pregnant after seven long years. The news transformed the whole atmosphere at home. Ma talked nonstop about her daughter and her yet-to-be-born grandchild. Vishal also expressed happiness in his own way; he called his sister up every week, though most of the time he spoke about the dismal unemployment scenario in India, and the job offers he was expecting.

Ma was elated at the thought of becoming a grandmother, but she was candid in expressing that she would have been happier if she were getting a grandchild from her son.

"I will give you my *Kundan* set when you give me a grandchild," Ma announced, stroking my hair.

I daydream:

Ma accompanies me to the gynaecologist for my monthly check ups. Vishal reminds me to take my iron tablets daily. He takes me to the washroom, holding me tenderly when I get the urge to throw up while eating dinner. He stands with me, massaging my back until I finish, then he wipes my wet mouth with a towel. Ma makes a variety of dishes for me and keeps telling me 'eat this, eat that, you need to eat for two.'

Ma gives me a Banarasi silk sari and a diamond necklace for my baby shower ceremony. "I want a healthy and normal grandchild, I don't care whether it is a boy or girl," Ma announces to a group of women at the baby shower ceremony. When the baby is born, Vishal carries the baby at night when she cries due to colic. Ma wakes up and offers to carry the baby for some time.

I knew my baby would be a harbinger of change for me; I would earn the respect that was due to me in the family, the respect reserved only for the daughter-in-law of the family. Vishal would love me like never before. The baby would melt his heart. It was sheer thrill to imagine that I could carry a human being in my womb. My graduation could wait, my dreams of being an RJ could wait; I convinced myself that conceiving at this stage of my life would be a blessing. Once the baby started eating the solid food, I could start chasing my dream. Anyway, Ma would retire in another few years, and then she would be able to look after the child while I pursued my education and took up a job. The self-talk pepped me up.

I prayed for a baby, and prayed very hard. But even before my prayers were answered, Kiran's pregnancy had changed the entire track of my life.

Ma was flying to the US for the delivery the following week; Kiran had already sent the ticket. That day Ma called me to her room after dinner and showed me a diamond pendant on a chain.

"How is it?" Ma asked placing the pendant in my palm.

The sparkle of diamonds dazzled me. It was a pea-sized magnificent oval of glitter, a small diamond in the centre, surrounded by six miniscule diamonds. I was overwhelmed by Ma's generosity. Ma was so happy at the thought of becoming a grandmother that she had wanted to gift me a diamond pendant. The luminous piece threw a cloak of amnesia around the memories of the fake jewellery gifted to me at the wedding. I felt a sudden pang of guilt for harbouring negative thoughts about her.

"Such a lovely design, Ma!" I exclaimed, my hands waiting impatiently to hook the chain around my neck.

"I hope Kiran likes it," Ma said, taking the jewel from my hand.

"And look at this one! This is my *Kundan* set; I wore it for my own wedding." She opened another velvet box. "Kiran is becoming a mother, so I have to give her something nice," Ma explained. "Look at the shine! The design is also antique; Kiran will love it."

Ma brought the necklace closer to my neck to see how it appeared on my bare skin. The same set she had promised me.

"Don't worry, I will give you a new one when you become a mother," she said when she saw the disappointed expression on my face.

My wounds turned raw again. I was reminded of the fake jewellery given to me. I could not bear the discrimination. Ma wanted her daughter-in-law to cook and do all the household work, but while distributing assets, she thought only of her dear daughter. I pretended to smile, but the radiance of the *Kundan* necklace had burnt my heart.

I ran into our smoky room upstairs.

Vishal was reclining on the bed, a cigarette in hand. He always needed nicotine to propel his 'thinking power'. He was in such a deep thought that he didn't even look up when I entered the room.

I stood at the edge of the bed and waited for him to notice me. I was fuming.

He looked through me.

"Do you even know what is happening in this house?" I shouted when he didn't acknowledge my presence.

He didn't stir.

"Are you listening?" I yelled again.

"What happened?" he asked calmly, bringing himself back from his thoughts.

"Ma is giving away her ancestral jewellery to her daughter. She has also bought a new diamond pendant for Kiran."

"So?" Vishal raised his eyebrows as he took another puff.

"Your sister is grabbing all the family jewellery and you sit here and smoke. All the jewellery Ma gave me for marriage turned out to be fake. I was given stones in the guise of diamonds, and now she is buying real diamonds for her daughter. Why this discrimination? I ask you, does anyone care for me in the house?"

I went closer to him and shook him roughly. "Why don't you tell Ma to give that set to me?" I screamed in his ears. My eyes were blinded by the glitter of the gold. Perhaps the *Kundan* set was just a catalyst; I spit out the venom that had been brewing inside me for a year; his fake degree certificates, his indifference towards me, his chain smoking, his unemployment and all the frauds committed by his family.

"If you won't protest, your mother will give the entire house to her and throw both of us out. You don't have a job; we need some security." I tried to reason through my rage.

Before I could open my mouth to speak again, I felt the force of his heavy palm on my cheek. Giving me no time to recover from his heavy blow, he slapped me hard on my other cheek.

I was horrified at his outburst. Covering my cheeks with my hands, I gave him a hateful glare through the hair strewn all over my tear stained face.

"My mother committed fraud? And what did your parents do? Gave me village dung wrapped in silk! How dare you speak like that about my mother? I told you earlier also... You bitch!" He slammed me against the wall.

I fell down with a thud, banging my head against the floor.

"If I were not a *manglik*, I wouldn't have married a rustic woman like you. It was a trap laid out by your bloody Pandit," he barked giving me a kick in the stomach. I could see anger and hatred etched on his face. He had fire in his eyes. He kept kicking and pounding me. My cries for mercy didn't move him.

The cigarette from his hand fell down in our scuffle. He picked up the cigarette and brought it near my face.

"I will burn your face if you ever talk like this about my mother or sister," he snarled. The cigarette was millimetres away from my face. I could feel the heat on my skin. Out of fear, I stopped crying and looked at him with pleading eyes, my face wet with spit and tears.

"You are inauspicious. First your baby brother died and now you will take my life." Giving me a dirty look, he left me on the floor and went to the balcony to smoke.

I had no idea how long I lay there with every muscle of my body aching. Small groans were still coming from the back of my throat. Every nerve of my body hated him at that time. I didn't know if the violence was his reaction to my bitter words about his mother, or the offshoot of his venom against me. In our one year of marriage, I could hardly recall any loving moments except at night between the sheets. He was always withdrawn and talked to me only in monosyllables.

After a few minutes, he came inside and stood near me.

I thought he was about to hit me again. I was in for a shock.

He knelt down and gently held my head.

"Get up from the floor," he said softly.

I obeyed, I was so scared.

"I am sorry, I was angry because you reminded me that I'm still without a job. I shouldn't have hit you, forgive me please," he beseeched. "You burn me with this cigarette, this is my punishment." All of a sudden, he thrust the burning cigarette in my fingers and pressed it to the back of his hand.

"Nooooo," I screamed, throwing the cigarette away.

I could never understand him. He could be a monster one minute and then turn caring and kind in the next moment.

Wiping my tear-stained face with the back of my hand, I got up to bring some Burnol and applied it on his wound.

"I am so sorry. I should not have provoked you," I kept repeating.

I didn't know why I always surrendered.

We were awake the whole night. He talked about his aspirations. I listened with my tear-stained face. I dared not interrupt him.

"I don't know what happens to me when I am angry; either I want to kill someone or kill myself," he confessed.

When he loosened up, he also told me all about his unhappy childhood, when his mother brought up both the children single-handedly without any physical or financial support from Papa. Apart from her hectic school job, Ma also had to give tuitions to make both ends meet. There were times when his mother would go in the morning and come back at night, leaving the young children alone at home. She was never there for them; it was always her school and her tuition children. He blamed his father for it. Ma had to work because Papa didn't provide financial support for the family. He had no fond memories of his father. His father was hardly around in his growing years.

"I want a homely wife who takes care of the house and children; I don't want my children to miss out on their childhood because their mother is busy pursuing her career. I don't want you to talk about becoming an RJ or anything else," Vishal concluded, dousing my dreams of becoming a career woman.

When I woke up in the morning, my body ached terribly. I tried to get up from the bed but my legs seemed to be tied in chains. The acute abdominal pain was unbearable. My entire body had a prickly sensation. I was barely able to open my eyes. I almost shrieked when I looked down with groggy eyes and saw that the part of the bed sheet below me was soaked in blood. I thought I had gotten my period, but when the pain didn't stop, I informed Ma. I was rushed to the doctor. I had had a miscarriage. I had a miscarriage and I didn't even know that I was pregnant.

Last night's incident had drained me of any emotions to react to my miscarriage. Getting brutally beaten by my husband or the miscarriage, I didn't know which was worst.

Ma wanted to postpone her trip to the US, but no tickets were available for the next one month; there was also a stiff penalty for cancellations. I couldn't be sure if she was concerned about her son or me.

A few hours before her flight, she called me to her room.

"Leela! Vishal has been suffering from deep depression since he lost his job," she told me without preamble. "He is otherwise a very lovable person, but he cannot control his anger. He's tried to commit suicide quite a few times before," she added, watching my face for my reaction.

I had begun to perceive everything with suspicion. Was Ma's sweet talk a ploy to trap me into something? I had become like a sponge, I could take in as many surprises.

"He has promised to me that he will never raise his hand on you again," she clarified. "Now Vishal is your responsibility, please take care of him and don't annoy or provoke him for anything," she pleaded, stroking my hair lovingly.

Overnight, I was forced to grow from a young bubbly girl into a responsible and mature woman. I had barely any time to mourn the death of my own baby, and now I was expected to be responsible for the life of someone else. My miscarriage had led him into another bout of depression. Ma left for the US, leaving me with the responsibility of a house, as well as her mentally sick son.

No one was concerned that my frail body had undergone a miscarriage and needed rest.

"If you had told me about your pregnancy, I wouldn't have kicked you." It was ironic that Vishal blamed me for our baby's death.

I didn't argue because not only was it futile, but I was also too scared to upset him. How would I handle it if he tried to commit suicide again? Or even hit me?

I hoped that all my miseries in life would end the day Vishal had a job in hand. I went to bed every night hoping that the next day would be that day. Finally, the wait ended.

CHAPTER 7

Bangalore

Infinite Pharmaceuticals was one of the top three pharmaceutical companies in India. The company manufactured life saving drugs and critical hospital equipment. Vishal was offered the position of an Assistant Marketing Manager at its Bangalore branch. The firm had its headquarters in Mumbai, with offices spread across all major cities of India. The company was planning to explore the South Asian market for exports. The plan to open a sales office in Bangkok was already in the pipeline. This job offer was nothing less than manna from heaven for Vishal, who had been unemployed for more than two years. The pay package was attractive, with a few perks attached. The only grey spot in the gleaming picture was relocation to Bangalore. Vishal had never stayed without Ma, but the options available to him at that stage of his career were nil.

"The first thing I want to do after reaching Bangalore is to buy a second-hand car," he announced emotionally. "Finally, I will be the proud owner of a four wheeler, a secret desire that every man cherishes."

I was pleasantly surprised to see him emotive. I was happy for Vishal, I was happy for myself, and I was happy for us. I wanted a new start to our life.

"Finally I am getting lucky because of you!" he said, putting an affectionate arm around my shoulders.

I smiled. Vishal had expected many good things to happen after his marriage to a girl whose horoscope matched perfectly with his, but when none of that happened, he didn't fail to taunt me about it whenever the opportunity arose.

I called Mummy and Pushpa di to share the good news with them.

"I will go to the *gurdwara* today to seek blessings for you." Mummy was thrilled beyond words.

"Leela, forgive and forget the past, start life afresh in a new place with your husband," Pushpa di advised. "I have a strong intuition that Bangalore will strengthen the bond between both of you."

Vishal and I left for Bangalore the next day. We were put up in the company Guest House for a month. Kiran had delivered a healthy baby boy. After Ma returned from the US, she visited us in Bangalore to help us furnish our two-bedroom apartment in a middle class locality. New furniture, new vessels, curtains and everything else that was required to start a new household from scratch were purchased by Ma. She obviously had no trust in my capability. She found my tastes too gaudy in comparison to her son's penchant for sober things.

"Leela, the new coffee brown sofas look excellent in your drawing room. Even if they are dark coloured, dust them every day, and listen! Wipe the glass table only with newspaper, don't use cloth; otherwise it will get scratched," Ma kept giving instructions until her train chugged away from the station. Ma was returning to Delhi after her two-week stay in Bangalore.

Vishal's eyes became moist as he waved to his mother.

Running a house independently was not as exciting as I had thought it to be. In Delhi, I only had to follow Ma's instructions, but in my house, I was responsible for everything. Vishal's new job involved a lot of travelling, but he controlled my life even while he was on tour. I was not allowed to step out of the house without his permission although he didn't mind me venturing out alone sometimes. I had to maintain a daily record of every penny spent. The brand of shampoo, the number of bathing soaps for the month, names and quantity of pulses to be purchased; he dictated everything. All I had to do was pay the amount and bring the things home in the auto rickshaw with no liberty to buy things that I wanted to. I noted everything in the blue diary, stapled all the bills and showed them to Vishal every Sunday morning.

Vishal carried forward his mother's legacy of controlling everything in the house including the clothes I wore, the menu for dinner and the neighbours I could mingle with.

His habit of beating me and threatening to commit suicide now and then had not gone. He would beat me when things didn't go good for him either at work or home. The shrill sound of my desperate cries when he pounded and kicked me echoed in my mind all the time. He would hit me with whatever he could lay his hands on – belt, umbrella or whatever. He travelled a lot which gave me respite from beatings. For the few days that he was in town, I would wake up every morning hoping and praying that the day would be a good one. I tried my best to keep him happy. We lived like a normal couple on those days when he didn't beat me but then something would always set him off. And of course it was always something I did, or failed to do, something I said or didn't say. It was always my fault. He said he gave me everything, a two-bedroom apartment, a car, good clothes, things I could never afford on my own; but I wanted none of that. Once while talking to my mother on the phone, I broke down and told her about Vishal's violent behaviour.

"This is extremely bad, he should not hit you. But don't worry; he will be fine after you have a child. He is a nice man otherwise. May be he has some work related tensions," Mummy said. "Try not to annoy him," she advised.

I carried out Vishal's commands without flinching. I didn't know what would invite his wrath. After every fight, after every physical abuse, he apologized and made me believe that he was really sorry for what he had done. For some time, it would be all fine, but then something would trigger and the cycle would start all over again. Swearing, calling me names followed by physical abuse and threats of suicide and then apologies. The same bruises, same promises, same him, same me. At the back of my mind, I continued to nurse a feeling that one day it would be all fine, the way it happens in movies...

Companionship and compassion, the two threads which bind any relationship, were missing from my marriage. Vishal was a very cold and self-centred person. He had no friends. Ma was the only person with whom he shared a warm relationship. A few hurried moments of tangled limbs between the rustling sheets occasionally, reinforced my marital status. For me, sex was just like yet another task because everyone did it. It was not something that I looked forward to. In spite of our efforts, I was unable to conceive again. Vishal still blamed me for the miscarriage. I wondered why so much of fuss was made over not having a baby. I had been married for three years, and was only twenty-two. I had my whole life left to have a baby. I was devastated when I had a miscarriage, but now I was happy that I had not yet conceived. I didn't want to bring up my child in a loveless atmosphere. It was ironic that after all the promises that I had made to myself, like my mother, I too, had a mute existence in my marital home. In fact, her situation was better than mine; at least her husband didn't beat her.

My parents had never visited me though they called me up sometimes. I would talk to them as if I was a normal, happy woman. I didn't discuss Vishal's behaviour much. My marriage to Vishal had uplifted me in my parents' eyes. Even if Sanjay was at home, he would never speak to me though he would call Vishal sometimes on his own to discuss share market. How much I wished that I could bridge the gap between us but perhaps like our parents, Sanjay too considered me inauspicious, and wanted to keep a distance from me.

My mind was gradually getting tuned to idle life; months flew past as I indulged in endless gossip sessions with my new neighbours, Sapna and Revathi. My spirit of adventure lay in forging grocery bills and using that money to watch first-day first-shows of movies with Sapna. I no longer felt guilty for leading a purposeless life and had reconciled myself to the fact that weaving dreams before marriage, and realizing them after marriage, were two opposites. I didn't remember the last time I had picked up a novel to read. I no longer got goose bumps when I listened to RJs. I had learnt to laugh with my mouth closed, as instructed by Vishal. I could also speak softly and didn't swing my arms while walking. I found solace in the fact that my marriage had helped me come up to a middle class status.

CHAPTER 8

Pushpa di called one day. "Leela, do you remember Priya? That tomboyish girl who lived in that corner house; there was a huge Jamun tree outside their house, the one who used to play cricket?"

I faintly remembered that petite cricket-crazy girl. In those days there were very few girls who thought of pursuing cricket as a profession, but Priya was different.

"Priya is a pilot, and she lives in Bangalore," Pushpa di informed me, reading out Priya's phone number.

Priya was ten or twelve years older than me, but there had been a kind of rivalry between us; something like sibling rivalry. The vibes between us ranged from neutral to negative but never positive.

I remembered Priya making fun of me. "What is this *jingbang* you are wearing? You look like a mobile bangle shop." She was vocal about her dislike of my noisy glass bangles, colourful clothes and penchant for making sure that everything always matched.

"Priya, bring some colour to your life, your life is so bland; you are always dressed in cricket whites," I retaliated.

Another association between Priya and I was that we would walk back together to our respective houses from the local bus stop every day. I, from school, and Priya from the cricket ground after six hours of rigorous cricket practice in the hot sun. With her face reddened from the heat, her feet thumping heavily on the tar road, her backpack swinging from one shoulder and bulky cricket kit from another, there was nothing feminine about her.

Priya's house was a few blocks away from ours, and on Mummy's insistence, she would often stop by at our house for a few minutes to drink a glass of cold water in the scorching heat.

"Priya, beta, one day when you play for the country, we will proudly tell people that Priya was our neighbour," Mummy would say affectionately.

Priya would smile demurely at that, fumbling for words to acknowledge the compliment, her eyes twinkling dreamily.

"Mummy, what's so great about getting selected for the women's cricket team? No one even knows about it!" I would mock after Priya left.

After a few months, Priya's father got transferred to Amritsar. Priya disappeared from my life, only to appear again in Bangalore after almost a decade.

"I thought you were crazy about cricket?" I asked Priya when I finally got her on the phone. Her phone was always either switched off, or out of reach. It was nice to connect with someone from my native place.

"Yes, I was, but I was crazier about flying. Cricket was the backup plan," Priya replied, her voice brimming with confidence. "Do come home sometimes. We are just the two of us, so mine is a very simple house," Priya said before hanging up.

A few days later, I visited Priya's 'simple house', which was actually a posh four-bedroom apartment in a plush locality of Bangalore. Chic sofas in pure black shimmery leather, silvery grey silk curtains covering the tall, sparkling clean windows, a small Persian carpet in royal blue, Raja Ravi Varma and M.F. Husain paintings adorning the cream walls; Priya's drawing room smelled of opulence. A crystal chessboard was kept on a huge centre table in rosewood with inlay work. A fifty-inch plasma TV on the centre wall completed the picture. I heard her mentioning the names of two actors from Kannada movies who happened to be her neighbours. It must have been so exciting for her to have celebrities as neighbours.

"What does your husband do?" I asked, admiring the Swarovski pieces in the showcase. I had seen them on a TV show on fancy homes.

"Leela,I am not married," Priya replied flatly, as she sank on the leather sofa opposite mine.

"Oh! Then who? You said 'two of us,' that's why I am asking."

"Why does 'two of us' always have to mean husband and wife?" She asked. "By 'two', I mean my four year old daughter and I," she said. "I adopted Hansa from an orphanage when she was a one year old baby," she added, before I could probe her any further on the matter.

Her young housemaid, Loveleen, interrupted us with fresh orange juice in crystal glasses, and something to munch.

"Leela, my father died of a heart attack while he was sitting at his desk in office. That day, it was my final interview for the pilot training course. While rushing to his office, I met with a near fatal car accident which almost ruined my chances of becoming a pilot," she said coldly. "You know, I couldn't even attend my father's funeral. I was struggling for my own life in the hospital," she added with a blank look and unemotive voice.

I listened with rapt attention.

How Priya could be so emotionless! I thought. Was it humanely possible to stay so calm and unperturbed while going through such personal crises in life? And why should a successful and good looking woman choose to stay unmarried, then throw all societal norms to the wind and adopt a child, when she could have had her own biological children! Did her family support her decision? How did her neighbours react, and how did the child feel? I had too many worries about Priya's life.

"So you will never get married?" I couldn't help quizzing her on the subject of marriage.

"Nothing like that, I will decide if the time comes. Now tell me about yourself." Priya looked visibly irritated at being asked too many questions. In spite of knowing that Priya was a private person, I couldn't help asking her about her personal life.

"It must be so glamorous to be a pilot," I said excitedly. I was reminded of my own dream of becoming a RJ. How I wished people could say the same about me!

"Leela, the grass is always greener on the other side. Everything that is not yours looks exciting and glamorous. The way other people sit in an office, I sit in the cockpit. I don't see any other difference."

"Doesn't your erratic work schedule disturb your biological clock?"

"It does, but that's an occupational hazard. Flying is a passion for me; I wouldn't trade that for anything else."

While she answered my questions about her life, her hands were busy checking out the mails on the table. She picked up an invitation card from the heap of old flyers and papers. She read the invite out aloud.

'Silver Wedding Anniversary

Cocktail and Dinner hosted by Mrs and Mr Avasthi

Hotel Oberoi'

"I get a lot of invites like this," she said passing the card to me. "You know, life is very strange. People call me for their parties only as a value addition to their dos. I generally refuse plainly, instead of inventing excuses for my absence. I only go where my daughter is also invited; I hate leaving her alone."

Priya called Loveleen and instructed her to set the table for two. Loveleen took out two table mats from the cabinet and started arranging the china on the table. "Hansa will be home in ten minutes. When I am at home, we have lunch together," Priya explained.

My face went pale. I understood that the second plate was for Hansa, and it was a subtle indication for me to leave. I expected her to ask me to join them for lunch, but she didn't. I might not have accepted her lunch invitation, but I would have appreciated if she had asked. Priya however didn't believe in courtesies, she had always been different.

When I was about to leave, a little girl entered the apartment, holding Loveleen's finger.

"Hey, here comes Mamma's princess," Priya exclaimed, her joyful expression at the sight of her daughter was conspicuous. Fair complexioned, pink lips like rose petals, small brown eyes, thick, long eyelashes and two pigtails framing her cherubic moon shaped face, Hansa looked exactly like Priya. Seeing them together, no one could believe that Hansa was not her biological child.

"Hansa, this is Leela aunty. Say hello to her. She is Mamma's friend," Priya said, introducing us.

Hansa didn't respond to her mother; she ran inside with her bag. She was out in a jiffy with a drawing book in her hand.

"Mamma, look! I did this in the class today," Hansa said putting her drawing book on Priya's lap.

"Wow, that's so beautiful, Hansa!"

The little girl smiled. Taking the file back from her mother's hands, she held it against her chest and stared at me. It was obvious that she wanted to show her drawings to me.

"Hansa, can I also see your lovely drawing? Will you show it to me?" I stretched my arms towards the child.

Hansa slowly walked up to me, still holding her file tightly against her chest, her eyes twinkling with the prospect of showing her creativity to a stranger. She handed the book to me from a distance, and before I could pull her towards me for a hug, she ran back to her mother. We burst into laughter at Hansa's clever act. Priya made the child sit on her lap. While I pretended to look at the squiggly lines in the book, Priya joyously listened to Hansa's day at school. She played with her daughter's tiny arms and hands as if she were a toy. The girl was a chatterbox. She was entertaining her mother with incidents about her school, the lunch break, homework and other things I was unfamiliar with.

“Okay Priya, nice meeting you, I will come some other day.” I got up to go. I was intruding into their little world.

“Okay Leela, thanks for dropping in. We will catch up.” Priya set Hansa on the sofa and got up to hug me.

Long after I reached home, I kept thinking about Priya. I wondered if it was possible to love an adopted child as much as your own. What kind of women were those who didn't want to get married by choice? Our science teacher in school was an unmarried woman in her mid-forties. If there was any requirement for additional duties after school hours, it was always Miss Urmil.

Our teacher hated it when her single status became an excuse for others to burden her with more work.

If she shouted at her students or argued with staff members, she was labelled a 'Frustrated Spinster.'

“Miss Urmil can't be soft with children because she doesn't have her own,” the high school girls argued.

I was thinking about Priya. If I were in her place, would I have the courage to ignore societal norms and do what I wanted? I questioned myself.

I couldn't find an answer.

CHAPTER 9

"One PPF form please," I asked the middle-aged clerk at the counter. Vishal had sent me to the bank to deposit the money. He would often dump such tasks on me on my weekly errands and I happily lapped up such opportunities. It gave me a chance to explore the city on my own.

"Madam, wait a minute, please." The clerk's voice sounded more like the harsh command of a military General. I noticed his forehead was adorned with three thick horizontal stripes of sandalwood paste. His military type voice didn't suit his soft religious-man face. "Madam, take the form." The man with the sandalwood stripes brought me back from his forehead.

I found a vacant chair against the wall. After filling the form, I went over to the counter and handed the money, along with the filled form to the clerk.

"Can you also update the passbook please," I requested. "My husband needs it to file income tax returns." I thought it was necessary to give the reason.

A few more people had come to the counter by then.

"I will finish with them first," he replied taking the form and the money from my hand. I walked towards the chair where I was sitting earlier. Someone else had occupied the chair. I looked around for a place to sit. I spotted a vacant chair outside the safety locker section. I occupied that chair and waited for my turn. I looked for some reading material to pass my time. There was none. One pink withdrawal slip had fallen on the floor. I picked it up. It was blank, except for the account number and the name of the account holder. I tried to read the name; I couldn't read because the handwriting was not legible.

"Excuse me," I heard someone call me.

I looked up.

A smartly dressed woman in a figure hugging lavender top and tight blue denim jeans stood in front of me. With a complexion of peaches and cream, well-shaped eyebrows, fluorescent lip colour in a shade of mauve on her small shapely mouth, she looked like a diva. Her dark brown hair, with a few streaks of maroon, was neatly tied into a bun at the nape of the neck, and not a strand of hair was out of place. Diamond studs, not flashy but big enough to be noticed completed the perfect picture. She was a head turner by any definition. A diamond on her tooth became visible when she beamed a smile at me.

"Leela Sethi?" she asked me.

I gave her a bewildered look. Who knows me by my maiden name in Bangalore? I thought.

"Are you from Government College, Patiala?" the woman asked when she didn't see any trace of recognition on my face.

"Remember me? Should I give you a clue?" she asked when she continued to see a lost expression on my face.

She didn't need to give me a clue. I had suddenly recognized the face. I stood up with a jolt.

We hugged each other as tightly as we could.

"You are in Bangalore, and I didn't even know!" Harleen said.

"If you are destined to meet someone, you will definitely meet, no matter what. But if you are not ordained to meet, then that person will cross your path at that very moment when you bend down to buckle your shoes."

"You are still philosophical, you haven't changed much," Harleen teased me.

"Not changed? I have put on so much weight." I unsuccessfully tried to grip my bulging love handles, which had formed a soft roll around my waist.

The rest of our conversation was punctuated by our loud laughter. It had been ages since I had laughed; I was amazed that I could still laugh so freely, and with my mouth wide open.

Suddenly time stood still. It was like nothing had changed and we were the same Leela Sethi and Harleen Kaur Chatwal studying in Government College Patiala. We could catch up from where we had left.

Harleen was four years my senior in college; she was in the final year when I joined. She spent most of her time in the canteen, sitting with her gang of friends, whose only objective in college was to have a good time, and a degree at the end of five years – three years of graduation and two of pre-graduation. Theirs was a very fun loving group. The other girls in the college envied them. The tall and lanky Harleen Kaur Chatwal was the most popular girl in our college.

We had nothing in common, really. She was a typical *Sardarni* – daring, vivacious and breathtakingly beautiful. I was just the opposite. I had always been in awe of Harleen. Even though she was not academically inclined, she was very popular amongst the students and the teachers. In a way, she was my role model. I wanted to be popular and daring like her.

CHAPTER 10

"Indiranagar, 1st Main, behind the market," I instructed the auto rickshaw driver as I jumped into the auto. Harleen had invited us for a get-together. Vishal expressed his inability to attend due to a sales conference in Hyderabad the same day. Even if he were in town, he wouldn't have agreed to go for a party; he hated socializing.

"You can go alone if you want to," he said before leaving for the airport in the morning. I didn't know if I had heard him right. He was allowing me to go to a party all alone; I couldn't believe it.

Covering my freshly blow dried hair with the black chiffon dupatta, I held on to the side of the auto for support. The auto driver manoeuvred his way through the evening rush. I could feel the smoke from the passing vehicles settling directly in my lungs.

"Stop... Stop here," I shouted waving my hand.

The vehicle screeched to a stop right in front of Harleen's bungalow. The forty-five minute auto ride on Bangalore's bumpy roads had crumpled my clothes. I stepped out and straightened the creases on my crepe salwar kameez. Thrusting two hundred and ten rupees in the driver's hand, I hurried my way into the house.

Harleen lived in a huge mansion. Four minarets in shiny marble around a vast porch big enough to park five or six vehicles, gave the house a palatial look. The colourful murals of women in myriad dance poses on the sidewall in the porch added colour and warmth to the entrance. There was a small fountain in the shape of a frog next to the gazebo. The water dribbling out of its mouth looked so nice. The child in me smiled. The sprawling lush green lawn, with rows of flowerbeds, made the place look refreshing. Harleen's house was an extension of her personality – bold, flamboyant and glittery. I had often seen such bungalows from outside, during my evening walks with Sapna, but I never had an opportunity to see them from inside.

The party was by the poolside in the backyard. The crystal clear water above the blue tiles of the swimming pool appeared serene in the backdrop of the vacillating coconut palms that lined the rear boundary of the house. Uniformed waiters sauntered around with trays of mouth-watering snacks in their hands. I had never been to such a lavish party before. For a moment, I thought I was there by mistake. I felt odd there without a man by my side. I played with the loose end of my dupatta to conceal my nervousness; I straightened the creases in my clothes again with the palm of my hands. I had worn my best salwar kameez in pure crepe, but in front of exclusive designer wear worn by high society women with hourglass figures, my clothes looked like house wear. Much to my relief, no one paid any attention to my ordinary clothes, stitched by a budget tailor on Magadi Road.

Harleen came running to greet me when she spotted me. She looked radiant in a pista-green Sabyasachi sari. The back of her blouse was held together by a thin satin cord with miniscule bells hanging from it. Seven strings of tiny emerald beads strung on a platinum chain sat neatly on her slender neck, making her long neck appear still longer. A diamond hair clip glittered on her neatly done chignon.

"Where is your husband?" Harleen asked.

"Vishal is on tour. He wanted to come, but couldn't make it." I was adept at making excuses for Vishal's absence. I didn't want to prolong the discussion about my husband. In a gathering of MDs, CEOs and owners of big businesses, I didn't feel comfortable talking about a husband who worked as an assistant marketing manager.

Harleen introduced me to some of the guests in the party. She left me with a group of elegantly dressed women and got busy attending to other guests. After exchanging a few pleasantries and talking about the weather and the city's increasing traffic woes, I didn't know what else to talk to them about. The women also didn't show any interest in engaging me in conversation.

"What would you like to drink? Would you like some wine, or would you prefer something else?" Harleen's husband Anand came to rescue me from the awkward situation.

"Nothing really, I am not thirsty," I replied, relieved to find someone I could talk to.

"You don't need to be thirsty to enjoy a drink." Anand laughed as he signalled the waiter to bring a soft drink for me. At this, a woman in a tiny black dress, standing in the vicinity, laughed spitefully but said nothing. I held on to my glass of coke tightly. I was scared that out of my nervousness, the glass might fall from my hand.

I looked at the grandeur of the bungalow. Out of the blue, my mind was enveloped by thoughts of Ranbir, my Patiala admirer. He was the only other person I knew who could afford to live in such a huge house. After his marriage to a girl named Ruby, he had constructed a massive bungalow. Theirs was the only house in our locality, which had a mini swimming pool. I had never been to his new house.

"Every day we see big cars parked outside their house. The entire neighbourhood cannot sleep the day Ranbir has a party in his house, the music is so loud." Mummy would often give me the neighbourhood gossip update. Sanjay and his wife, Bindu, were sometimes invited to Ranbir's parties.

I daydream:

I am married to Ranbir. We are the richest and the most popular couple of Patiala. I have a car and a driver to myself. We love to throw parties at home. People feel privileged to be invited to our parties. Draped in a pista green Sabyasachi sari, I am giving instructions to the waiters and looking after the guests, just the way Harleen is doing.

"Madam, would you like some *Seekh Kabab?*" The waiter transported me back from my dream world.

The DJ was playing music at full blast. One by one the guests started moving to the makeshift dance floor around the pool.

I watched Harleen and Anand dance to a slow number. How lovely and madly in love they looked!

Harleen's metamorphosis from a rustic belle to grace personified had bowled me over. Wow, what luck! I thought. Harleen had a seven-year-old son who studied in a boarding school in Ooty, but she still looked like a teenager.

"How does such a small child live without his parents, so far away in the hostel?" I asked her when she told me about their son.

"He is not small, he is going to be eight and I meet him thrice a year." She smiled. "Leela, good education is important for children. You will know when you have your own. Forget it, now, we must meet often, not after ten years," Harleen said cheerily when she came to see me off at the gate.

"Sure, next time in my house," I blurted out, but then wanted to eat my words. I pictured Harleen sitting in my middle class apartment. There were two sofas in coffee brown, whose upholstery had never been changed, three cane chairs and a centre table in cheap wood. Ma had purchased the chairs from a roadside furniture cart. A few threads of cane had come off the chairs, which Vishal had fixed with Fevicol. Straight pieces of cotton cloth, hung from aluminium rods, were called curtains.

The darkness permeated everything when I reached home. It was pitch dark everywhere except for the scattered patches of light emanating from a few apartments with their own inverters. Usually there was only a one-hour power cut in the evenings, the timings would vary every day, either it was from six to seven, or eight to nine. Six to seven was manageable as men were still at work and most of the women were out in the park with their children, or strolling on the narrow jogging track in the apartment complex.

I fumbled with the house key, struggling to open the lock of our apartment. I didn't mind the scheduled power cuts; that's how the life was with everyone in our building, but today the dark night looked gloomier than usual. Perhaps I was blinded by the glamour of the 'Page Three' party I had just attended.

From a high profile party to a house full of darkness, it was like Ranbir's curse had come true.

"Leela, you will never be happy without me," he had once said.

That night I tossed and turned in bed. Harleen's opulence had reminded me of my own middle class existence. Marrying Vishal, I had scaled up the social ladder, but I was still a poor middle class woman in comparison to Harleen and Priya. How small and timid I looked in front of Harleen and her friends! Harleen was a rich socialite and Priya was a successful career woman.

"What's my identity?" I questioned myself.

"Unhappy, frustrated middle class woman who gets beaten by her husband," I mumbled.

I could have been living in a house as big as Harleen's if I had agreed to marry Ranbir. Perhaps it was my destiny to marry Vishal and come to Bangalore. How happy was I when my alliance with Vishal was fixed! I had declined Ranbir's proposal without a second thought, thinking I would be better off marrying an educated and cultured man. A cultured man who treated his wife like a piece of crap, I mocked. For sure I wouldn't have become an RJ if I would have married Ranbir, but I would have lived like a queen. And more importantly he loved me a lot. God was perhaps punishing me for rejecting true love.

CHAPTER 11

Harleen's life was an enigma to me. I was curious to know more about her affluent life - what she ate, where she slept, where she bathed; I wanted to feast my eyes on her luxurious lifestyle once more. After two days, I landed at her bungalow, unannounced and uninvited. The aroma of expensive perfume, mixed with the smell of tobacco, filled my nostrils when I entered the bungalow. A ladies' kitty party was going on.

"Meet Sheila, Liz, Suhan, Kalpana, Seema, Malika… and this is Leela, my college friend from Patiala." Harleen was elated to see me. I thanked heavens.

After a quick round of introductions, everyone got busy in what they were doing earlier. A game of housie was on and thousands of rupees were at stake.

"Why don't you also play?" Seema asked me.

"No, I am not very good at it. I will watch you people." I made a quick mental note of the money in my purse before saying this.

I caught Kalpana and Liz exchanging a snide smile. "What is there to be good at Housie?" I heard someone murmuring in undertones.

Amongst designer wear georgettes and pure chiffons, my cotton salwar kameez in bright yellow looked like rags. I felt everyone's eyes were on my ordinary clothes, the thin gold *mangalsutra* around my neck, my artificial earrings and glass bangles. I didn't sit for the fear my clothes would wrinkle. I stood there holding Harleen's chair.

Harleen thrust a glass of red wine in my hand before she got busy counting notes on the table. I had never tasted alcohol before. Vishal would kill me if he came to know that I was drinking.

"I don't drink, I will take orange juice," I kept saying.

"Today you will have to drink; you didn't take anything in the party the other day," Harleen protested.

I accepted the glass reluctantly. I took a small sip. I didn't like the taste, it was too sweet. I took another sip of the wine, letting the alcohol wet my throat. I was unable to decide whether I liked the drink. Wine was the drink of the rich and famous. The tall glass of wine in my hand made me feel rich, like the rest of the people in the room. I took another sip.

It's not that bad, I thought.

From the corner of my eyes, I observed the women in the room, the way they had held their glasses. Seema was the most stylish in the group. The glass rested on her palm, the stem between her fingers; her thumb and the tip of her index finger touching the glass on either side for support. She took the glass to her lips to take tiny sips of wine. Avoiding everyone's gaze, I slipped the glass down to rest on my palm and held it between my finger and thumb. I took the glass to my lips to take a small sip. I moved my eyes around to see if anyone was watching me imitate Seema. No one was; they all had their eyes glued on their housie tickets. I was beginning to relish the wine now. I didn't say no when Harleen offered to refill my glass.

"Ela! How have you come?" Seema asked me, taking a puff of her cigarette. I liked the way she slowly puffed the smoke out of her mouth.

I was not sure if Seema had gotten my name wrong, or whether it was too old fashioned to be pronounced in the chic ambience. I didn't bother with the reason. I liked my new name. It suited the atmosphere.

"My car driver dropped me off," I lied boldly.

Later I realised everyone had shortened names. Harleen was Leen, Suhan was Su. Mohini was Moh. With my short name, I too had joined the group of stinking rich women.

"Do you like Bangalore?" someone asked.

"Actually I ..."

"Hey, I am going to South Africa next week," Kalpana interrupted us. Harleen's friends were soon engrossed in their conversation, forgetting that I was about to say something. I listened to them attentively, nodding my head now and then in affirmation to what they were saying. I parted my lips in a smile when they laughed at something funny. I thought I too was expected to smile. I tried to be a part of the group. I didn't have much to add. I remained quiet most of the time. I feared they might laugh at my middle class status, but they didn't, at least not in front of me.

"Mohini, are you sure, you can handle one more?" Harleen asked when Mohini wanted a third refill of Scotch.

"Yes, I can handle as many as I want," Mohini replied taking a large gulp of her drink.

The women were all ears when Mohini spoke. No one moved, no one went to the veranda to take a puff, no one got up to take a helping of spicy snacks or take a refill. Mohini provided them with enough spice for the rest of the party.

"You know," Mohini looked at Suhan and said, "The first time I started drinking Scotch was when I found my husband in bed with my friend. She calls herself my friend, but she is a bitch stabbing a friend in her back. And my husband is mad after her. When he tells me he is going for a client meeting, I know who the client is."

"What are you talking about?" Suhan asked in defensive tone.

"You bloody bitch, I am no fool," Mohini hissed.

Everyone turned their necks to look at the two women pouncing on each other.

When the situation seemed to be going out of control, Harleen summoned her secretary, Jenny.

"I am sorry to have spoiled your party," Mohini said while leaving.

"You have actually made our party," someone said. The words were followed by a loud giggle.

"Hey ladies, the party is still on," Harleen announced when she came back after escorting Suhan and Mohini to their respective cars. "Let's have another game of housie; this time 2,000 each ticket. First house 10,000."

The women got busy piling crisp notes on the marble table.

"And the winner gets Seema's handsome husband for one night as a bonus," Kalpana announced loudly, resulting into roars of whistling and giggling by the women. Seema, too, joined in the laughter.

I was baffled by their talk. It might be dirty talk, but it was carefree and fun. Seema didn't look surprised that her husband was being used as enticement in a simple housie game. She was in fact smiling the most, her almond shaped eyes twinkling at the mention of her husband's name. Probably it was a compliment. These women might be modern by Indian societal norms, but they were still nice. They didn't make me feel small. Unlike me, they were not bored housewives who had nothing to do to pass their time. Most of them were busy working women. Seema was an art curator - I had never even heard of this profession. Liz was an educational consultant, Suhan was a jewellery designer and Mohini had her own event management company. After meeting them, I realized that I was so out of touch with the new world.

"Suhan is a jewellery designer, and makes more money than her doctor husband," Harleen told me.

I listened to their happening lives. They didn't ask me uncomfortable questions like what my husband did, which car he drove, where I lived and other such questions. Although they hadn't bothered me much, deep within, I was disturbed.

CHAPTER 12

"Hi Leela!"

I was pleasantly surprised to hear Harleen's singsong voice at nine in the morning. We had not spoken to each other after the kitty party in her house fifteen days ago. I had called her once but she was in a spa at that time.

"*I vil cal u back,*" she had texted, but she hadn't.

Vishal had left for Mumbai by the early morning flight. I was still lazing around when Harleen rang up.

"I am going shopping. It will be nice if you can give me company," she said.

I was thrilled at the prospect of shopping. I felt privileged to be invited for a shopping spree by a rich woman who bought only designer stuff. Harleen had many stylish friends, but she had chosen me to accompany her. I ignored the thought that all her fashionable friends might be busy, and that I was the only one who was totally jobless.

Shopping is so much fun when spending is not emptying your own pocket. I jumped out of the bed to get ready. We were to meet at the entrance of Shoppers Stop. I decided to reach earlier than the scheduled time. It was not that I was particular about punctuality; I just didn't want to alight from the auto in front of Harleen.

Harleen arrived in her chauffeur driven BMW an hour after I reached.

"Hi Leela, thank you so much for coming." Harleen hugged me.

She was wearing a pink half-sleeve v-neck T-shirt with black capris. A pair of chic sunglasses was perched on her head. The short T-shirt revealed part of her seductive midriff.

Harleen had come prepared with her shopping list.

"I want to buy only traditional wear today. I buy my western clothes from the US," she said.

After browsing for an hour, she shortlisted eight salwar suit sets.

While Harleen tried on her dresses one by one, I stood outside the trial room with the rest.

After trying on each dress, she would ask my opinion. I shared my thoughts for each one. Frankly, everything looked nice on her. Of the eight, she selected six.

After ethnic wear, we went to the household section. She picked up a few bed sheets and cushion covers as gifts. She kept prodding me all the time to buy something. I was tempted, but I had to practice a lot of self-control. I could not afford to buy from expensive stores. Finally, I decided to purchase two hand towels, worth four hundred rupees. The same thing I could have bought from any local shop, for less than half that price, but I had to buy something to save face in front of my spendthrift friend. Harleen was a quick shopper and knew her mind. Within two hours, she was done. If I were in her place, I would have taken all day to select this much of stuff. I volunteered to carry a couple of shopping bags for her. We walked out holding the bags. It felt good to be carrying heavy shopping bags containing expensive things, as if they were mine.

After shopping, we went to the food court on the top floor. Since I was new to the place, I let Harleen lead me. I had never been to posh restaurants. We hardly ate out. Vishal had to eat out during his travels so when he was in town, he insisted on eating home cooked food.

"I am so damn hungry," Harleen said, dumping the bags on two vacant chairs. We were dead tired; she of selecting, and I of carrying stuff that was not mine.

Harleen ordered pasta and a fresh lime soda for herself.

"How about you?" she asked me passing on the menu card. My eyes were glued to the right side of the menu. After scanning the price list for each item, I chose to go with a vegetarian sandwich combo worth two hundred rupees.

"Anything to drink, madam?" the waiter asked.

"No, I have a bad throat," I replied.

I was tempted by the image of a tall glass of chilled cold coffee on the menu card, it looked so real, but I had to content myself by licking my lips. I couldn't afford to spend one fifty rupees just on coffee. While eating, Harleen talked about her son. I was not listening to her. My mind was occupied; I was debating whether I should offer to pay for the lunch.

Would she ask me to go dutch, the way we did in college, when we divided every paisa spent, or would she offer to pay? Ideally, she should pay because I was only accompanying her for her work, but what if she expected me to pay for my own lunch! In that case, my bill would be two hundred rupees only, which I could manage, I thought.

In my mind, I was cursing her for coming to a place where a sandwich worth fifty rupees was sold for four times the price.

"Let me pay." I pretended to open my purse when the waiter brought the bill.

"Today's lunch is on me. I made the programme." Harleen snatched the bill from my hand and handed over her credit card to the waiter even before I could open my purse.

I was relieved. I had only one five hundred rupee note in my purse, after having been forced to spend four hundred on the hand towels. If I knew she was going to pay, I would have taken something cold to drink, at least a fresh lime soda; I was so thirsty.

Harleen went to the restroom to change as she had decided to go to the *gurdwara* after the shopping, and capris were not appropriate to wear to a religious place. She was back in ten minutes wearing her new salwar kameez, and glowing as usual.

Her driver pulled the car right in front of us when we came out.

"Should I drop you?" Harleen asked dumping her bags in the boot.

"No, thanks, my driver will be here any moment," I lied.

CHAPTER 13

I'd had a hectic, but fulfilling day. I had gone shopping with a rich socialite and she had appreciated my tastes. At least, that's what she told me. After a quick wash, I made a cup of lemon tea and plonked on the sofa. It was bliss to have a steaming hot cup of tea after a hectic day. It quenched my daylong thirst. By the time, I finished half the mug; my body had absorbed the warmth of the tea. I was already relaxing. I wondered if Seema felt the same when she smoked out slowly.

Before going to bed, I opened my shopping bag to take out the towels I had purchased. I was worried about the explanation I would have to give to Vishal for my indulgence. These days he was so engrossed in his work that he hardly observed anything, but I had to be ready with an excuse just in case. When I dug into the bag, instead of the towels, out came Harleen's pink T-shirt and capris, the one she had worn during the day. The clothes reeked of expensive perfume. I took her T-shirt near my face, to smell it, to feel it, to soak in the richness that it had absorbed. I had the sudden urge to try her clothes on, and see how they looked on me. I took off my nightgown and slipped into her clothes. The T-shirt was a bit tight, but the capris fitted me well, except for my small paunch. I pulled my stomach in to make my abdomen look flat. The tight

T-shirt made my bosom appear voluptuous. The exposed midriff was sensuous. I looked like a young college girl. I had never worn western clothes. Before marriage, Daddy ji didn't allow, and after marriage Vishal didn't approve of it. Short kameez and Patiala salwar with a flowing dupatta had always been my signature style.

I opened my braid and let my silky black hair fall over my shoulders. One long curl fell over my forehead to flirt with my dark eyes. I pulled back my hair in a high ponytail and stood at an angle to see how my side pose looked. With hands on my waist, I stared intensely at my image in the mirror. I didn't look like a plain Jane from Patiala. I looked like someone else, someone who was confident, who knew her mind, who was desirable and beautiful. Seeing my new look in the mirror, I smiled. My soul smiled.

I opened my hair again and let it fall all over my face. I took out red lipstick and applied it on my lips. I pouted my lips and brought my face closer to the mirror. I kissed the mirror; then I kissed the image of my lips on the mirror. It was sensuous. I opened the drawer and took out a cigarette from the pack – perks of having a chain smoking husband. I held the cigarette in between my lips, lit it and took a puff. I exhaled the smoke slowly like Seema. I took another puff and watched the smoke billow from my mouth. It was rising above, magically. I was staring at the smoke. How a cloud of smoke vanished in air leaving nothing but an intense stench. I was alone. I was myself, untainted, unquestioned, the purest form of my being, doing what I wanted to. It was the most fun I had ever had in life, and the sense of power I experienced was something I had never felt before.

Getting more adventurous, I went around the house looking for something more exciting to do. The house suddenly felt like an unexplored land full of surprises. I opened Vishal's cupboard and found a bottle of malt whisky hidden behind his books. My curiosity grew when I spotted another bottle of liquor. I lifted a few more books and found bottles hidden behind the books, most of them still unopened. Vishal rarely drank, but he liked to collect liquor bottles. His hobby didn't make sense to me. I was surprised he had stocked so many of them over the years.

Oh, it was a full-fledged pub here, I mean bar, I corrected myself.

Whatever…

Vishal had once explained the difference between a pub and a bar to me, but I always got confused between the two. I only knew the common factor between them was alcohol.

There is a natural curiosity to taste the forbidden. My lips quivered as I tasted the first few drops from the bottle. I hadn't expected it to be so bitter. I didn't know if it was the taste of alcohol, or the dust on my fingers.

I dipped my finger in the bottle and licked it. Red wine had tasted better than whiskey, but I wanted to try this one out. Experimenting was the flavour of the night.

I quickly brought a glass from the kitchen and poured whiskey in it. I sipped it slowly. Sitting on the rocking chair with the glass held tightly in between both my hands, I bounced on the chair, my hair flying all over. I didn't relish the taste of alcohol but I liked the taste of adventure. I loved the feeling of the glass in my hand, it made me feel important.

I smiled. I had entered a world full of hope and happiness. I looked at the bottle of whiskey and gave a contented smile.

I poured a few big drops again, and then turned the glass upside down in my mouth.

Enough; too much is bad, I scolded myself.

I dozed off on the rocking chair, in Harleen's clothes.

"I don't want them back, you can use them, I have worn them so many times," replied Harleen when I called her in the morning. "I am sure they will fit you. I will send your towels through my driver."

"They should fit, but I will try them on and text you," I lied. I didn't want to tell her that I had been sitting in her clothes and drinking all night.

"Yes, they fit me, thanks," I messaged after four days.

Instead of sending her driver, Harleen came over to my house. She had brought a few of her old T-shirts, two pairs of jeans, a designer handbag and one pair of bright red Jimmy Choo shoes.

"I am bored of wearing them; you can use them if you don't mind," she said empting her bag on the table.

Of course, not, I wanted to say, why would I mind free designer stuff? Instead, I said, "you know Harleen, I like to wear simple clothes but maybe they would be good for a change. I am not sure, you can leave them here, I will see."

"They are almost brand new. I have worn them only once," she said when she observed me eyeing her Jimmy Choos greedily. "Actually they are a little tight. I think I purchased one size smaller by mistake," she added.

The stuff was as good as new, except for the handbag which had a small tear, but that could be mended by a cobbler in fifty rupees.

Looking admiringly at the expensive heap in front of me, I shooed my self-esteem away and accepted her second-hand gifts. No one could say that the items were old after all.

Gradually I became her dumping ground for discarded stuff. I didn't mind one bit. I had new additions to my wardrobe, the things that a middle class woman like me could only dream off.

The shoes were tight for me as well, but I somehow managed to fit into them. Revelling in my prized possession, I passed them off as gifts from Harleen when Vishal asked me about it.

CHAPTER 14

Revathi's teenage daughter, Chethana, had agreed to teach me the basics of computers. I was excited. I was about to commence my journey into the cyber world. The seed for my tech voyage was planted at Harleen's house last time, when Suhan was compiling everyone's email IDs to send out invites for her exhibition. She asked for mine too. I was not sure whether she asked me out of courtesy, or she really wanted to invite me. When I didn't open my mouth for a few seconds, she asked me to SMS my email ID to her. There was no possibility of me texting her as I didn't have an email ID at all. I felt I lived in the ancient age, still scribbling on paper. Vishal had an old computer at home that had been gathering dust for a long time; his company had given him a sleek laptop to carry his office with him everywhere.

I had never used a computer before because I didn't know how to use one. I had asked Vishal to teach me how to send emails but he always shrugged me off. "What will you do? To whom do you want to send emails?" he had asked me.

Chethana was computer savvy, like all youngsters.

"Chethana, I don't know anything about computers," I confessed when she came.

"No issues, Aunty, it's very easy. Even a child can learn," she said, trying to encourage me.

She explained the functions of the various parts of the machine. And then she created an email account for me, 'Leela.chopra@gmail.com', teaching me how to send emails, attach and download documents, how to search for information and related stuff. It was all very simple. I inaugurated my email ID by sending an email to Harleen.

Dear Harleen, please send my email id to Suhan. Note it down; my email id is leela.chopra@gmail.com. Thank you, yours faithfully, Mrs Leela Chopra

Chethana laughed when I showed her the email before clicking on the send button.

"Leela aunty, you don't need to mention your email ID in the body of the email. It is going from your ID so it is already there."

The use of the word 'body' for a lifeless thing like email was amusing. In any case, I removed my ID from the body.

"Aunty, these days a functional knowledge of computers is a must for everyone, even a housewife should know. I keep telling Mummy to learn, but she says she won't do anything with it. I appreciate your enthusiasm at this age."

I didn't want to tell her that I was just five or six years older than her. I only looked like I was in my thirties.

I practiced my lessons every day and within no time, I was bored of sending test emails to the same set of people – Harleen, Chethana, Sanjay, I was sure they too were bored. Harleen and Chethana at least replied to my emails. My brother never even bothered to acknowledge it. Vishal was right; there were not many people to whom I could send emails. I prodded Chethana to teach me something interesting which I could practice more often.

"Do you want to open a Facebook account?" she asked.

"Yes, sure," I replied. I had heard about Facebook but didn't know what it was. The entire world was using Facebook, why shouldn't I?

At that time, little did I know that an activity, which I just thought would pass the time, would change the entire course of my life!

Leela Chopra, Status – Married, City - Bangalore. Facebook was very user friendly. I learnt how to send and confirm friend requests, search for friends, upload pictures and to write on people's walls. I was free to scribble whatever I wanted on my own wall. With the click of the Enter key, my writing was visible to all my friends; it was nothing less than a magic to me.

Chethana was my first friend. I sent friend requests to Harleen and all her friends. After I was done, I sent the requests to all their friends then friends' friends and so on. I sent friend requests blindly; some accepted while some didn't. I wanted to have lots of friends; I wanted everyone to know me. I also received friend requests from unknown people; I accepted all. Harleen had 1811 friends; I wanted to have more than her. I observed people's walls and imitated them. My updates were usually about what I cooked for dinner or which movie I watched on TV. Announcing my personal life to strangers didn't make sense to me, but that's what I saw on everyone else's walls. I had already lost enough opportunities in life; I didn't want to be left behind in the race. I wanted to tell the world that I was a modern woman, a woman of today and not a naïve woman.

Within a month, my friend list had crossed a hundred. Most of them were strangers whom I had never met, and would never meet, but still they were my friends. I changed my profile picture every week. I searched for school and college friends. I remembered only a few names. Sushma had cleared her IAS and was posted as deputy commissioner of Ajmer. Rashmi was a professor of Economics in Canada. Lata was a bank manager in Delhi. Vishal didn't know that his old computer was in working condition and that it was being used to expand my social circle. I logged in every two hours to check updates on Facebook. Buying an internet stick was not a problem. I had enough money from my housie games.

My moods varied with other people's updates on their profiles. I would become unhappy to see others' happy faces. All the women I knew were having a good time with their families and vacationing in exotic locations; I was the odd one out; the one whose husband didn't have time for her. There was nothing exciting happening in my life. Every time I logged in, I became aware of my shortcomings. I had nothing to boast of, no foreign or Indian vacations to show off, and no smiling pictures with my husband or anyone else.

In spite of such heartache, I revelled in my newfound ability. I loved the feeling that I was in the same league as the rest of the world.

CHAPTER 15

Harleen often invited me to her parties. Vishal accompanied me only once and then too, he didn't make any effort to talk to people. He replied in monosyllables when someone tried to strike a conversation with him. His body language conveyed that he was feeling out of place.

Anyway, I loved going to parties, with or without my husband.

Courtesy Harleen, I had the experience of eating in fine restaurants. Now every other day Harleen would pull me to a different place - places I could never afford to visit on my own. And of course, she insisted on paying the bill every time. I didn't mind. I could construe only two reasons for her affinity towards me. First, like me, she, too, wanted to connect with someone from her hometown. Second, she wanted the satisfaction of showing off her wealth to me. I had now become a part of her group. Though I was not rich like them, the group seemed to like me. They invited me for all their kitty parties as a guest. Sometimes they had get-togethers in fancy restaurants, where the women went dutch. I gave all such parties a miss. I didn't miss the parties hosted in someone's house; they were, of course, free.

Harleen said it was very important to network and have a good circle of friends; you never know who would benefit you when.

Though I didn't meet Priya often - she was always busy either flying, or with Hansa - I was happy to be connected to her. Priya called me sometimes while on her way back from the airport. I loved talking to Priya, even though it was mostly Priya who did the talking. I adored the feeling that I was talking to a pilot, an independent career woman whom society looked up to with respect. When I met Sapna and Revathi in the evenings I would narrate to them, dialogue by dialogue, the conversations I had had with Priya and Harleen. It gave me a high that I knew rich and famous people. I didn't want to remain a village belle all my life. I wanted to be called a hip Bangalorean, just like Seema, Mohini, Priya and Harleen. I had also learnt how to play housie. I won the first house when I played for the first time. I couldn't believe it; I went to the party with one thousand rupees in my purse and came back with twelve thousand. Everyone had to pay two thousand rupees for the game. Harleen offered to pay on my behalf when I informed her that I forgot to go to ATM before coming. I had a new excuse each time I didn't have sufficient money.

"Thanks. I will return the money to you later," I promised.

"Don't worry, you enjoy now." Harleen smiled.

Harleen knew about my economic status as she had come to my apartment a couple of times; perhaps she realized every time I lied to her but she never said anything. When I returned the borrowed money to her, she refused to take it back, even though I insisted a few times. I left it at that. So what was the big deal if she didn't take the money back? It was a very small amount for her.

CHAPTER 16

Harleen called to invite me for a coffee morning at her house.

"Leela, don't be late, otherwise you will miss the demo session on waterproof makeup."

I had a terrible headache that day and had gone to sleep after sending Vishal to office. I was in no mood to venture out, but didn't want to miss an opportunity to learn free makeup tips along with a good sumptuous meal, and a chance of winning another full house.

Jasmine was a beautician by profession. She was also the franchisee holder for Flairs, a new cosmetic company. She had come to promote her products, and to make a killing by selling exorbitantly expensive cosmetics to rich women.

"I need a plain face where I can demonstrate how Flairs can transform your looks and give you a complete makeover," Jasmine said with a fabricated smile and a snooty accent.

I was the unanimous choice, as everyone else wanted to watch the demo. I, too, had come to learn something new and didn't want to sit there with my eyes closed, but I didn't want to offend them. I still harboured the feeling that they indulged me by including me in their group. I agreed to be the guinea pig. I was made to sit on a chair in the centre of the room. Jasmine named the products and its benefits as she applied them on my face, neck, eyes, lips and hair. My eyes were closed so I could not see what was being done to me. I could only hear the women giggling over something. I didn't know if the joke was about me or something else, but it was a heady feeling that for two hours all eyes were fixed on me. I was enjoying all the attention and fuss over me. I also heard the sound of cameras clicking.

When I opened my eyes, I was welcomed by the sounds of their enthusiastic appreciation and praise.

Was I really looking beautiful?

Blemish free complexion, sharp dark eyes, skin like porcelain, a shapely nose, a seductive pout on my kissable lips; I could not believe it. I had never experienced such admiration before. They all had their own versions of which heroine I resembled - Rekha, Madhuri, Deepika. I didn't know which film star I looked like, but I definitely didn't look like Leela Chopra.

The women were all charged up. They asked me to pose for their cameras. I obliged. I loved every moment of it. It was not enough; the women wanted to have more. Harleen quickly brought a few of her dresses and commanded me to wear them. One by one, I tried everything on - saris, a mini skirt (thank God I had waxed my legs!), leggings and jeans. I walked with a swing to my step like a model on ramp. Everyone cheered me. The cameras flashed again, accompanied by the sound of applause.

I felt like a celebrity. Thanks to Harleen, I was living my dream- if only for a little while.

“I will email the pictures to you,” Harleen said, seeing me off. She asked her driver to drop me. “You are looking so lovely, someone will whisk you away and your husband will ask me where his pretty wife is!”

I laughed because this could never be true, not a stranger whisking me away, but Vishal calling me pretty.

I didn't want to wipe my makeup off. I wanted to surprise Vishal with my new look. I waited for Vishal to come home. I didn't move around much, thinking that my makeup would smudge. When the doorbell rang, I ran to open the door. Vishal entered and went inside to change, without saying a word to me.

“Here the entire world is complimenting me, and this man doesn't even acknowledge my new look.” His indifference saddened me.

“So how was your day?” I asked just to bring his attention to my face.

“Okay,” he replied without looking at me. He looked tensed.

“How do I look?” I asked him directly.

He looked in my direction. He gawked at my face and paused for a moment before opening his mouth to speak.

“What have you done to your face?” he asked with a hint of irritation.

“Do I look nice?” I smiled.

“You really want to hear how you look?” he asked after a long pause.

“Yes, of course!” I beamed from ear to ear. I waited for him to shower me with compliments and then carry me in his arms and take me to the bedroom.

"You look like a bar girl, a girl who dances in cheap pubs where drunkards ogle at women," he said grabbing me by the arm and raising his hand to hit me. "Do you want to hear more? Do you?" He screamed, shooting a hateful glance at me. "Next time I see you with paint on your face, you will be out of my house; I really mean it, you whore!" he barked, clenching his fingers to control himself from hitting me.

I stood in stunned silence. Tears of humiliation welled up in my eyes. I couldn't understand the ruckus over my makeup. I walked up to the washroom to wash my face. The cotton swabs were soaked with dry makeup and tears.

CHAPTER 17

Vishal had already left for office when I woke up. I tried not to think about the previous night's incident and busied myself cleaning the cupboards. Household chores didn't interest me. How long could one go on folding clothes?

Pushing them aside, I switched on the computer. The computer was old and took a long time to start. I logged in to Gmail to check my emails. I hardly received any emails but you never know. My eyes sparkled when I saw an email from Harleen. Apart from the usual messages and notifications from Facebook, this was my fourth email since I had created my email account; the earlier ones were from Chethana and Priya. Harleen had sent my pictures, which had been clicked yesterday. This was an instant mood lifter. It was amazing to see how makeup could transform one's looks completely. I appeared so different from my real self. For a moment I thought those were not my pictures, but it was me of course - the same Leela, just with makeup and borrowed clothes. I gazed at my photographs intensely; my smile widened each time I looked at them.

My mood changed. I logged into Facebook. I commented on the pictures of strangers, liked their posts, and wrote 'I am bored' on my wall. Liz had uploaded the pictures of her recent trip to

Netherlands. Madura Dam, tulips, cities with unpronounceable names, all those names were alien to me. How I wished I could also have such lovely pictures to show to the world. At that moment, an idea struck me. I didn't have pictures of foreign trips, but I did have some nice pictures to share with my friends.

A wicked thought crept into my mind when I was about to upload my pictures.

After two hours of trial and error, a brand new profile appeared on Facebook. *Name - Elaa Singh, Status – Single, City – Delhi, Profession - Student of Mass Communication.* I had liked the name given to me by Seema; I decided to add an extra 'a' to it. It was not that I believed in numerology; it was just fashionable to add one extra letter to your name, the way celebrities do. Elaa was conspicuous and made me stand out amongst the commoners, just like my pictures. After much deliberation, I zeroed in on one picture in which only half of my face was visible. A thick black lock caressing my forehead, mischievous eyes, small nose, flawless skin, high cheek bones… I looked bewitching; I was not sure whether it was the magic of Jasmine's brush or Harleen's expensive camera. Jasmine had requested me to take off my *mangalsutra* before applying foundation on my neck. At that time, I was offended, but I was now happy to see my neck without any strings.

I changed my profile picture every day. It was fun, but there were no comments or likes on my wall. I had no admirers for my new look. I was disappointed; it had been fifteen days and Elaa didn't have a single friend request. But then, how could she? She didn't exist. What was the use? I wondered how Harleen and her gang would react if I sent a friend request to them. Would they recognize me? I didn't want to send friend requests to people

I knew as this was my secret; I didn't want to share this with anyone, not even with Chethana. What if someone informed Vishal!

After two days, I was delighted to receive one friend request from a terrific looking boy, Manoj. He was a student of Economics in Mumbai. I wondered how he found me. I accepted the friend request. What was the harm anyway? I was only indulging in some harmless fun. Manoj commented on my pictures. I replied to his comments and messages. I was glad I had some traffic on my profile. I started getting friend requests frequently; mostly were men, young and old. I accepted all requests. I, too, started sending friend requests to strangers. All of them accepted. My pictures and credentials were too attractive for anyone to reject me. I laughed when I compared Elaa with Leela. When Leela sent a friend request to someone, the chances of accepting were only ten percent, but everyone accepted Elaa's friend request. It is rightly said that everyone wants to be friends with successful and beautiful people. In a month, Elaa had surpassed Harleen's friend list.

I had a few students of journalism as my Facebook friends. I studied their walls and copied the content on my wall, with minor alterations to make them look genuine. *I am going for advertising class, new American student in the class today; PR assignment was very interesting;* all the posts were copied. I wanted to show to the world that I was a smart woman, and not dumb like Leela. Whenever I wrote something on my wall or uploaded a picture, a 'like' appeared within seconds. I had twenty of those pictures; I was still left with two. The people left flattering comments about my pictures. *You are lovely, can we meet, beauty queen, I am crazy about you, sexy, you give me sleepless nights, a stunning beauty.* I laughed.

I loved the adulation. My admirers were real people who were being fooled by a fake girl.

It was fun and day by day, it was becoming more exciting. I knew I would never be caught by Vishal. He still didn't know that his wife was putting his ancient computer to good use.

Ma was arriving the next day. I had been slogging in the kitchen since morning, making a variety of dishes. She always came during her summer holidays.

"Your friend Priya called, she wanted to speak to you," Vishal informed me when I came out of the kitchen after finishing the groundwork for the dinner.

"Hey Priya, how are you?" I called her when Vishal was taking a nap after lunch.

"I am okay. Just wanted to talk to you," Priya didn't sound like her usual contented self.

She informed me that Hansa's biological mother had surfaced from nowhere and was laying a claim on the child.

"That woman calls me every day; she wants to meet Hansa. Leela, I am worried. She is coming home today evening."

"Priya, you have not kidnapped Hansa, you have adopted her legally, so you need not worry," I comforted her.

"Leela, it is not that simple. What if Hansa wants to go back to her biological mother?" Priya explained, her voice just above a whisper. "Leela, can you come home in the evening? I want someone to be with me when that lady visits me," she requested. Priya had no family in Bangalore.

Vishal listened with indifference when I told him about Priya.

"I think I should go, she needs someone to be with her," I told him when he remained quiet for some time.

"What will you do? Can you help her in any way? This is her problem; let her solve it, why do you need to interfere?" he said politely but firmly, leaving no scope for any further arguments. Then he gave me a lecture on why adoption should be banned, why adopted children could never be happy in their adopted homes, and why parents could never accept someone else's child as their own.

"I think it is better if you leave her alone and let her decide what she wants to do. Today I am at home. Tomorrow Ma is coming; you should focus on your own household responsibilities instead of interfering in others' lives," he advised. "But anyway it's your choice."

The phrase 'your choice' always meant 'no' in the dictionary of our marriage. I kept debating in my mind whether or not I should go, but didn't have the courage to argue with Vishal. I didn't want to risk annoying him. He might not say anything to me right away, but he would definitely take it out on me some other time. I didn't want to create problems for myself during Ma's visit.

"Maybe my going will weaken her resolve." I tried to justify the guilt in my mind.

CHAPTER 18

Ma's six - week visit passed peacefully without any fights or arguments. I was relieved when Ma left. I hadn't met either Harleen or Priya for a long time. I felt so disconnected from the outside world. I was also disconnected from my virtual world when Ma was here. I logged in the day she left. I was not interested in boring Leela. I logged into Elaa's profile. There was a lot happening in Elaa's life. She was a celebrity for those nineteen hundred and thirty seven friends. Since Elaa was a virtual person, I could write anything on her wall. The more I indulged in it, the more I believed that Elaa was real. All my hours alone were spent on Facebook now. I didn't have the time to meet Priya and Harleen anymore; I was busy. Elaa gave a purpose to my life. Harleen had called me yesterday and I didn't take the call - I was uploading my pictures. *'I m busy, vil cal u later,* 'I replied in a text.

The more I loved Elaa, the more I hated Leela. I detested Leela for being submissive. Why couldn't the wimp gather up the courage to resist her abusive husband? I had divided my brain into two parts, one for Leela and one for Elaa. There was a fence between the two, and I made sure that neither of them trespassed into the other's area. I was enjoying the game. In one moment, I could become a married conventional woman, and in another a terrific looking career woman. I laughed. My life was a roller coaster ride. I really believed I was Elaa. How nice it would be if I could become Elaa in real life! Elaa was my alter ego; I wanted to be her; smart, good looking, confident, an independent person, and very popular. I was realizing my dream of being famous through Elaa.

Jai was one of Elaa's Facebook friends. He seemed to be just another young, average looking guy. There was nothing exceptional about him, which drew my attention to him. *Status - Single, Age - 28, City – Mumbai, India.* Apart from the brief bio-data, his profile didn't contain any other information. He had never commented on any of my pictures or wall posts. One day I was pleasantly surprised to receive a message from him.

Hi Elaa, I have been your silent admirer. You have a very photogenic face and I am sure you are the delight of every photographer. Can't help looking at your pics every time I log in.

Jai

I read the message once and then twice and then again. I was impressed by the words 'silent admirer.' It sounded very romantic. It was thrilling to receive such a compliment from a complete stranger.

Silent Admirer… I mumbled to myself.

Thanks, I replied. I didn't want to sound as if I had never received any compliment before. I wanted to keep conversation to a minimum. Elaa's male friends often gave cheap comments like; *Hi Beautiful, sexy woman, you are my dream girl, you are perfect, I want to kiss your lips, bewitching eyes, can I have your cell number* and what not. I would have a hearty laugh when I read them.

These Romeos would have a heart attack if they came to know that their dream girl was only a dream, and that she didn't exist at all. At that time, I didn't know that the joke was really on me.

The next day, while I was reading the comments posted on my wall, the chat window popped up. My silent admirer was online.

BTW what do you do? Jai typed in the chat box.

What did I do? I was a housewife, what else could I do except cook, and look after my house?

I am a student of Mass Communication in Delhi. Polytechnic College, final year. I replied when I realized that the question was for Elaa and not Leela. I didn't know the names of colleges in Delhi. I was not even sure whether such a college existed in Delhi.

Hmm. What plans after this? Visual or print media.

In between - I want to become an RJ, I want to become famous.

Wow, that's great! Oh, I am sure you have a lovely voice, just like your face.

Yes, I do. My friends say I have a smiley voice. When I speak, people think I am smiling.

I felt stupid sharing my dreams with a complete stranger. I gave a light slap on my forehead for forgetting my boundary.

RJ for becoming famous? Aren't there more interesting ways of attaining fame than becoming an RJ? You are more suitable for a model, you have a beautiful face!

The debate ended soon. I went offline. I knew I would goof up if he continued to ask me about the course I was doing, the subjects I was studying and related stuff. I could not go on lying endlessly.

Next day when I logged in, Jai was online.

Hi, RJ He typed in my chat box.

Where are you working? I asked him to divert his attention from talking about RJs. I had to prove that I could also quiz him. I waited for him to reply. I waited for the chat window to blink again. After a few minutes, he went offline.

It was like slamming the door on someone's face.

How dare you do this to me? I shouted at the screen. I wondered why he ended the conversation abruptly. Did I offend him in any way, or did he find out that I was lying all through? Was he having a laugh at my dream of becoming famous? Now I was not only angry, I was also embarrassed at my eagerness to befriend a stranger.

Out of curiosity, I clicked on Jai's profile. He didn't have too many of his pictures, and didn't seem to be Facebook addict like many other people. Most of his pictures were group pictures with friends, or people who looked like his family members. He hadn't updated his wall for quite a while. I shut down the computer, soaking in the compliments that my silent admirer had previously showered on me. I liked the phrase 'silent admirer'. It had an excitement, a kind of suspense around it. On the flip side, I was regretting chatting with a complete stranger. Was he a fake like me? What a cute, youngish name he has kept for himself! Revathi had told me about many cases of old, perverted men disguising themselves as young, handsome men and cheating young women. The world was full of such cons. I was glad I had the sense to not reveal my personal details to him. Gosh, it was dangerous!

CHAPTER 19

I slipped into my *jutti* and went down for a walk. It was already five. My neighbour Sapna was waiting for me. We set off on our regular route. I walked in silence; Sapna was telling me about a TV serial she had watched last night but I was not listening to her. I was thinking about Jai. My silent admirer had opened his mouth at last.

Next day, on our usual walk Sapna narrated how Chethana had a boyfriend whom she met over Facebook and how he turned out to be a married man with two children.

"World is full of liars and cheaters! This internet thing is so dangerous," she mumbled.

It scared me. After much deliberation, I decided to delete my fake Facebook account. Chethana had taught me how to create a new profile but she hadn't taught me how to delete one. I looked for any instructions or a delete button. I could not see it; maybe it was right there in front of me, but I could not see it in my nervousness. I was not at all nervous when I created the fake profile, but I was so damn nervous while deleting it that my hands were shivering. While I was trying to find out how to delete the profile, my chat window blinked. Jai was online.

Hi Elaa

Hi I typed after thirty seconds. One last chat perhaps.

Tell me, what else do you do apart from dreaming about becoming an RJ?

I was embarrassed all over again to have spoken about becoming RJ. He was making fun of me.

Are you coming to Delhi any time? I asked to distract him from talking about RJ.

I visited Delhi last year. I had come to meet my girlfriend.

My curiosity grew stronger once I found out that he had a girlfriend. Subconsciously I had already developed a soft corner for him. While I chatted with him, my eyes searched for the delete button. I wondered why I was chatting with him when I had decided to delete my account.

Your girlfriend, where is she now?

She is in Mumbai now; she works for an ad agency.

His status said single. Though I was new to the world of social networking, I knew the difference between single and committed.

You have a girlfriend but your status says single.

Do U want me to be single or committed?

Now he was flirting with me. A girlfriend in tow and flirting with a stranger, how typical of men!

Shut up, I don't care whether you are single, committed or married.

Don't get angry. Actually we have common friends; she doesn't want anyone to know about us so I have to keep my mouth shut.

By now, my eyes had stopped looking for the delete button. On the spur of the moment, I decided that I would not delete my fake profile right away. I promised myself that I would not log in at all. Why should I delete it? Not logging in was as good as deleting.

Tell me more about yourself. I found myself typing.

Within the next ten minutes, I knew everything about this stranger who was now an acquaintance and was on his way to becoming a friend. He had landed his current job even before he finished his education. When he was doing his Bachelor's in journalism, he was offered the job. He dropped out and joined Mumbai TV. He provided backstage support to the newsreaders and interviewers. Most of the time, he wrote the entire news script for the newsreaders. He said he could help me find a job if I was interested in journalism; he had many contacts. He was the younger of two brothers. Both his parents were doctors and lived in Sri Lanka. His elder brother was thirty-one years old and was still unmarried. Too much of information maybe but it established his credibility.

The conversation ended but I entered into a dream world.

I daydream:

I am reading the news in the newsroom of the studio. Dressed in soft peach full sleeve shirt and blue blazer, my eyes are fixed on the reading screen in front of me. The camera is capturing me from front. Jai is standing behind the camera, with a few sheets of paper which I will need for the 9 p.m. chat show. Mumbai news has invited two business tycoons to the studio today. I will be interviewing them. I am nervous because this is the first time I am interviewing someone on TV.

Jai raises his hand in a 'thumbs up' gesture, and cheers me up. Everyone is watching me on TV. Daddy ji proudly tells the relatives, 'Our Leela is a newsreader; she appears on TV every day.'

Jai was different from other men. Unlike my other male friends, his messages didn't have any sexual overtones. After complimenting my pictures initially, he never wrote anything about how I looked. Our chats revolved around his job, and what I wanted to do in life. He never asked me anything personal. He had drawn a line between the two of us. It might be because he had a girlfriend. Surprisingly, he hadn't asked for my phone number. Was he playing hard to get? I was confused. The more I thought about it, the more confused I became. Was he a fraud like me? By then I had dropped the thought of deleting Elaa's profile. Jai could be my medium to reach my destination. He was entrenched in the industry and surely had some good contacts, which could be of use to me at the right time. Now I was daydreaming with open eyes. I was so blinded by Jai's assurance that he could introduce me to some people in this industry; it didn't occur to me that sitting in Bangalore, my chance of landing a job with a TV channel in Mumbai was nil. Elaa could have still managed it but for Leela, it was far beyond her reach.

I shut my mind from Jai's thoughts and turned it to the real world. It was time for Vishal to come home, and I better behave like a woman who has only housework on her mind. I took the raw vegetables out of the fridge and got down to cooking dinner. I grated the bottle gourd, mixed gram flour in it, and one by one slipped the small round balls in the *kadai* to fry the *koftas*. The phone buzzed when I was frying the second set.

CHAPTER 20

My sister-in-law Kiran's husband, Navin, was coming to Bangalore for two weeks. He worked as a research analyst in the US. He often had to travel to South Asian countries because of his work. It was his first visit to Bangalore after we shifted here. Before this, I had met him only twice, once at our wedding and second time, when he had come to Ma's house in Delhi. My interaction with him had been limited to exchanging pleasantries and talking about life in general during dinner. From whatever I had heard from Ma and Vishal, Navin was very courteous and a fun person to be with. Being the daughter-in-law of the family, it was my duty to make his stay comfortable. We had stocked the house with bottled water, cans of coke, rolls of toilet paper, and such other things that people abroad can't do without.

Ma called up every day to dictate the menu for dinner, and the next day's breakfast. She wanted to ensure that her son-in-law was looked after well.

"Leela, our school is hosting a science fest; I am unable to take leave. Otherwise I would definitely have come."

Navin was an ideal guest. Unlike Ma and Kiran, he was not fussy about food, and other things. He would leave in the morning and return home in the evening. Sometimes Vishal picked him up on his way back. His visit didn't disturb my routine. Harleen's kitty parties, my Facebook friends, my afternoon naps, and the evening walks with Sapna, I could carry on with my routine as usual.

The two weeks passed quickly. It was time for Navin to return to the US. I was happy that I had been a good host to my husband's relative. Vishal had a sales conference coming up in Delhi and he could not afford to miss it. He apologized to Navin for not being there until his departure.

Vishal left for Delhi by the early morning flight. Navin too left home soon after; he said he had to meet someone at the Indian Institute of Science. He was leaving for the US the next day. There was a heavy downpour the previous night. It was all slushy on the roads when I had gone to fetch *Paneer* from the corner grocery store in the morning. Ma had instructed me to make *Paneer Makhani* for dinner.

The month of July in Bangalore is like November in Punjab, when the summer is over and the winter yet to set in, when the light woollens come out of iron boxes, spreading the mushy aroma of dry neem leaves everywhere.

It was still drizzling. Droplets of water glistened on the windowpanes like crystals. I opened the window and let the rain wet my stretched arm. The lush green trees in the park looked magnificent in the rain. I loved the clatter of rain when it fell on the leaves before hitting the ground below. The onset of rain signalled happiness to me. Back home in Patiala, the rain signalled onset of piping hot *Pakoras* and steaming hot cups of tea. I had hardly made *Pakoras* after marriage. Vishal stayed away from the oily stuff as far as possible and it was too much of an effort to do elaborate cooking for one person alone.

Thinking of *Pakoras* made me feel hungry. It was the perfect weather to have a cup of ginger tea. I went to the kitchen and made myself some tea. Cupping the mug in my lap, I settled myself on the couch near the window. It had started pouring heavily. Little splashes of rain fell on my feet. It was already afternoon and the sky was grey with misty air. I was still sitting near the window enjoying the rain with my fourth cup of tea, when there was a knock on the door. I was in no mood to get up, but I forced myself to answer the door.

I was surprised to see Navin home early.

"I have to go to Delhi this evening. I thought I would spend some time with you before I leave." He walked in.

"The weather is also nice to enjoy a cup of tea at home," he said giving a mischievous smile as he occupied the sofa in the drawing room.

"Oh, sure." I got up to make tea.

"There is no hurry, you finish yours first," Navin said, gesturing me to sit.

I smiled uncertainly before lowering myself on the couch, and taking another sip from my cup.

"Leela, do you know something?" he said, his eyes staring at the geometrical design on the cheap synthetic carpet below.

"What?" I looked up from my cup.

"You are so different from other women. Vishal is very lucky," Navin said, locking his eyes on mine. "How can he leave his wife and be away for weeks?"

"He has to. His work demands it," I said, feeling an unfamiliar need to defend Vishal.

He laughed. "You are not only naïve, but also very nice. Kiran would never let me go alone; she tags along with me everywhere. This is the first time she is not accompanying me on my travels abroad. You are an ideal woman, I envy Vishal."

I was surprised; Navin travelled a lot in connection with his research and Kiran never went with him. She had her own job. I felt his eyes on my breasts.

"Did you have your lunch? Should I make something for you?" I asked, trying to escape the uncomfortable silence, and his ogling.

"No, I am not hungry, but can I have some tea now, with more milk and two spoons of sugar, please?"

I was relieved to get an opportunity to escape. He was behaving strangely. I walked to the kitchen and put water in the utensil, waiting for it to boil. When I turned to take out the milk from the refrigerator, I noticed him leaning against the kitchen door, his arms folded across his chest.

"I am sorry to bother you," he apologized when our eyes met.

"No problem." I managed a smile.

He stood at the kitchen door and indulged in small talk.

I answered his questions in monosyllables, my back towards him. I continued preparing tea and shifting vessels unnecessarily to avoid turning towards him. I didn't like the way he was staring at me.

"Are you scared to be alone with me?" he asked, sensing my obvious discomfort.

I didn't know what to reply to him.

Why was the tea taking so much of time to boil today?

"Why aren't you talking to me properly?" he asked.

"I am preparing tea, I am busy," I said without turning, my head bent over the stove.

"Are you too busy to even look at me?" He asked, placing his hand on my shoulder.

My back was still turned towards him. I felt his hand caressing my shoulder and going up and down my bare arm.

His audacity stunned me.

"What are you doing?" I shook his hand away.

I turned away, pretending to be busy, hoping he would take the hint and leave. For a few seconds I did not hear any sound. I glanced over my shoulder; he was still standing at the door. I continued arranging washed vessels in their respective places, without a word. After I finished, I took an onion and placed it on the chopping board, wanting to do something to avoid looking at him. I didn't know what had come over him.

Before I realized what was happening, he grabbed me from behind and squeezed my breasts tightly.

I was aghast.

He jerked my face around and pressed his lips against mine, his tongue prying open my mouth. Without taking his lips off mine, he pushed me towards the wall, his body pressing against mine. I tried to push him away, but he was unshakable. I began to suffocate. He thrust his hand under my kameez, running his hand on my bare back. With the other hand, he squeezed my breast so hard, I whimpered in pain. His hands were roughly travelling all over my body, pinching me, pressing me. I felt the blood draining out of my head.

"Leave me, leave me please," I cried, as he paused to drag in a shuddering breath.

The phone rang. After a few rings, it stopped. It rang again, the tone sounded louder this time.

Navin winked and released his grip. I ran to answer the phone.

"Where were you, why you are not answering the phone? I have called you three times on your cell, idiot!" Vishal shouted. "The cell phone is not given to you to keep in your purse."

I was too terrified to open my mouth.

"Is Navin back? What time is his flight tomorrow? I am not getting through his number; something seems to be wrong with the network. Ask him to call me when he returns." He disconnected the phone without letting me say a word.

I was still shivering with fear. My throat went dry. There was darkness in front of my eyes. This couldn't be happening to me. Such things happen to people you don't know. Clenching the receiver in my hand, I looked back at the place where Navin was standing. He wasn't there.

Moments later, he came out of the guest room wheeling his suitcase, and laptop bag swinging from the other shoulder. He was leaving! I sagged in relief.

He stopped in front of me. He winked when our eyes met. My heart pounded in trepidation. He pulled me closer, sliding his hand inside my clothes.

I stood still, too scared to move. I wanted to shout, but my voice stuck in my throat. I wanted to run outside, but forgot which direction the door was in. I could not move; my feet were glued to the ground.

I felt him push me down on the couch and tug at my clothes.

Then I passed out.

CHAPTER 21

The buzzing of the doorbell woke me. I tried to get up, but my quivering legs and aching muscles pulled me down. I didn't bother to answer the doorbell. The room was dark. I stretched my hand to switch on the light, and looked at the clock with half closed eyes. It was eight p.m.

The events of the last few hours played in my mind. The incidents were coming in bits and pieces. I tried to recall what happened after Navin pulled me closer. I felt dizzy even thinking of it. Suddenly I experienced severe tightness, then choking sensation in my throat. I managed to walk to the kitchen to get some water to drink. The milk that had fallen on the floor had dried; the whole kitchen smelt of sour milk.

Fear, shame, guilt, anger, anguish... various emotions competed with each other to overpower me. I came out of the kitchen without drinking water. Like a mad person, I went from room to room in search of something. I didn't know what I was looking for.

I lay down on the bed and stared at the ceiling, my eyes wide open, the entire sequence of incidents replaying as a flashback, one after another. I forgot what happened first, how it all ended, what time it was. Did any of the neighbours see anything from the kitchen window?

How will Kiran react when she finds out about her husband's character?

What if Vishal tries to harm himself after knowing about this incident!

Thinking of all this, my head throbbed. The incidents played in my mind as the tears from my eyes fell all night. Too dazed to cry my heart out, my tears were like the drizzle outside: neither pouring nor stopping.

I was in a dilemma about confiding this to Vishal, but I knew I had to. Vishal returned after three days. I was surprised to see Ma with him. Her visits were always planned; she would announce about her visit months in advance.

"Ma was feeling lonely so I brought her with me for a few days," Vishal told when they entered. The flood of tears broke open once again on seeing a human face. I didn't want to cry in front of Ma; she would be heartbroken to know about her son-in-law's character but I could not hold back my tears. Neither Ma nor Vishal bothered to ask me the reason. For the past three days I had forced myself shut in the house; I had neither answered the door, nor phone calls.

That night when I was alone with Vishal, I told him everything.

"You should be ashamed to say such filthy things about my brother-in-law! Damn it, he is my sister's husband," bellowed Vishal.

"Ashamed? He should be ashamed of such an obnoxious act," I shouted back.

Vishal's reaction blew my lid off. I had expected him to at least sympathize with me, if nothing else.

"I don't believe a word of what you are saying. You are lying. Why didn't you call me immediately and tell me everything? Why after three days? I think there is something else at the bottom, which you are hiding from me," he said giving me an accusing look. He lit a cigarette and puffed at it furiously. "No, this can't be true," he said under his breath.

I was devastated by Vishal's reaction.

"I am not lying, Vishal, really, I am not. I was so upset, I didn't even know whether I should tell you all this."

"Then why are you telling me now?" he barked.

He paced up and down the room, exhaling thick smoke from his mouth vigorously to control his anger.

"Navin is a very nice guy. I knew him even before they got married, they had a love marriage. I still don't believe you. And don't tell this to Ma, she will throw you out of the house," he warned giving me a dirty look, as he paused to light another cigarette.

The door was pushed open.

Ma barged in. Without saying a word, she rushed like a storm and slapped me.

"How dare you say such dirty things about my son-in-law?" She was furious. "Kiran will be so hurt if she finds out about this. You look very innocent, but you have a malicious mind, I can vouch for Navin's character. May be you provoked him."

I was dumbstruck to hear Ma's words.

I looked at Ma, and then at Vishal. He was looking away, puffing vigorously. He stood there, immune to his mother's outbursts.

I stared at him through the blur of tears. His indifference enraged me.

"Get out of my house, you bitch!" Ma pulled me by the hair and dragged me towards the door.

Suddenly Vishal intervened, realizing that the situation was deteriorating with Ma's intrusion.

"Leave her Ma; I will speak to her later." Vishal pulled Ma's hand from my hair.

"What Later? You are sympathizing with her? Sympathizing with a characterless woman? I don't want to stay in your house even for a minute. Book my ticket right now; I am going back to Delhi." Ma shrugged off her son and stomped back to her room.

Vishal followed Ma. After five minutes, he was back.

"Ma is going, just because of you. Why did you have to create a scene? Couldn't you just keep your dirty mouth shut?" snarled Vishal. "No one listens to me. Ma is adamant, you are adamant. Both of you are making my life hell. I will leave both of you and go. I don't want to live." He banged the drawers of the dresser frantically looking for something. Before I could react to his threats and comprehend what he was doing, he cut open the packet of mothballs kept for the woollens, and tossed a handful in his mouth.

"Stop! Vishal, what are you doing?" I forgot my own agony and ran towards him. But by the time I reached him he had swallowed quite a few. In our scuffle, a few spilled on the floor.

"Ma! Ma! See what Vishal is doing, stop him," I wailed as loudly as I could, trying to snatch the rest of the mothballs from his hand.

Ma came running. She snatched the remaining mothballs, forced open his mouth, and made him vomit.

After Vishal had steadied himself, he threw a look at me, which conveyed that I was always the reason for spoiling the peace of the house. He directed Ma to her room holding her by the shoulders. Ma was sobbing.

I had expected him to console me, tell me to deal with it bravely, assure me that this too shall pass. A few words of sympathy would have calmed my strained nerves, but I was declared the culprit.

I broke down. I was assaulted by a double-edged weapon. I cried until there were no more tears left. My sobs finally trailed away, leaving a death like silence at home.

I dialled Pushpa di's number with trembling hands. I wanted to talk to someone who would sympathize with me.

"Don't you read in the newspapers? 99% of such cases are by a family member only, someone who will not be a suspect."

I had to call Mummy. I could not hide this from her. She had to know.

"Such things keep happening in families. There are bigger issues and still women keep quiet. They have to adjust, where will they go? People will talk about hundred things. You cannot run away just because your husband questioned you. Have you thought about that? It is ridiculous to even think of breaking your marriage for such a silly reason," Mummy said.

"Is this a silly reason?" I shouted at her on the phone.

"Beta, Navin's act is worth condemning, but what has Vishal done? Poor guy! Have you thought what he must be going through after listening to this? It's not easy for men, either. It doesn't mean that he is accusing you for this. And what if he would have swallowed the mothballs? What would your life be without him? It's a very cruel world. Can a woman live alone? Even if Vishal and his mother wouldn't have blamed you for this, does it change anything?"

Vishal's trust in me would have made a world of difference to me. I would have conquered any mountain if he was with me.

"Don't ever talk to your Daddy ji about this. He is a heart patient," Mummy said before hanging up.

I visualized Sapna talking to the women in the building; 'Leela was raped by her brother-in-law. And what did she do? Was she raped or was it an attempted rape? Where did he touch her? It couldn't have happened all of a sudden. He must have given some hints before; why didn't she tell anyone about it? He had been staying with them, may be they developed mutual liking and now she is putting the blame on him to save herself.'

Ma left for Delhi the next day. She said she was very upset over this incident. I didn't care. I had lost all respect for her.

I didn't have it in me to end my own life so I had no choice but to carry on with life. Just going through the day was an uphill task. I had barely any energy to cook a basic meal for Vishal. Lakshmi, the cleaning lady, had taken two weeks off to go to her village; anyway, I didn't want to see anyone's face.

I would be in my nightwear throughout the day with the house in mess, beds unmade, vessels unwashed, kitchen stinking. I avoided Vishal. I withdrew completely. The moment he reached home, I would feign a headache and get under the blanket, my tears soaking the pillow.

"Why are you lying down on the bed all the time? Are you sick?" Vishal asked me one day.

I didn't reply. I turned my face the other side and closed my eyes.

He tried to appear normal, but this incident had widened the crack between us.

"So, when is the next party at Harleen's house? I will surely come with you this time." Vishal made another attempt to break the ice between us.

I didn't feel the need to answer him. I swallowed a sleeping pill and took a sip of water from the glass kept on the side table before sneaking under the blanket again.

Lying down next to me, he put his hand on my waist. He entwined his leg between my legs allowing his other hand move freely all over my body. He slathered kisses on my back and kept murmuring under his breath. I knew what was coming next. Vishal didn't take no for an answer. I had understood the consequences of saying no. I lay still, like a corpse. I didn't resist when he turned my face towards him and started unbuttoning my nightgown.

"I hate you and I hate myself for allowing you to do this to me," I kept repeating in my mind until he finished.

He didn't see much change in me when he returned from office in the evening, the next day. I was still the same, lying in bed, my eyes swollen after crying the whole day.

"Now enough of this drama, you are not a newly married bride to behave coyly like this. Forget it now, it is over. Ma has gone back; she didn't want to stay here and for your sake, I didn't stop her. Is that not enough?"

I got up and stared at him for a moment and then started howling like a child.

"I can't forget it, I can't. I can never be normal again."

He let me cry. When I was done, he moved closer to me.

"Close this chapter now, let's not talk about it," he said softly. "I promise such a thing will not happen again. Now get back to normal and look after your house. Everything is messed up, I can't find my things. The food cooked by you is tasteless these days. Sometimes there is no salt. Sometimes there is too much. My clothes are not ironed. I have two sales conferences coming up. I can't sit with you all the time and waste my time over a trivial thing."

A trivial thing? I stared at him through a blur of emotions.

If hate could be measured, at that very moment, I hated Vishal more than Navin. All these years, I had been living in a world of illusion. An educated boy, a respectable family... was this a cultured family? Was it my fault that Navin molested me in my own house?

"How are your friends, Priya and Harleen?" he asked.

"They are busy, they have work to do," I shot back.

"Why don't you also do something to pass your time? Join some part-time job, there are so many things to keep you occupied for a couple of hours every day. Just look around, something will catch your fancy. You always wanted to become an RJ. Why don't you find out more about it or join some vocational course?" He opened my palms and entwined his fingers in mine.

I kept nodding to what he was saying. My heart was devoid of any feelings for Vishal. It was his way of doing damage control after committing the crime. He wanted a functional house where I could facilitate a normal life for him.

"You have to move on with life," he said, caressing my arms.

I listened carefully to what he was saying. His words made sense. I had to move on with life. My fate was bound to Vishal's. If my life was hell with him, it would be no better without him, I reasoned out. I could not be spending my entire life crying and paying for someone's mistakes.

"You need a purpose in life." Vishal's words echoed in my ears as I wiped the fresh tear that trickled down my cheek.

Chapter 22

Next morning Lakshmi reported for work. Gouri, her four-year old daughter walked behind her. Lakshmi entered the kitchen and got busy in piling up the dirty dishes in the sink. There were dirty utensils in the kitchen all over; I had not cleaned the kitchen counter after making dinner last night. Lakshmi was a chirpy woman in her late twenties. Dressed neatly in a cheap colourful nylon sari, her hair adorned with a twig of jasmine flowers, black beaded *mangalsutra* peeping out from her low cut blouse, Lakshmi looked every inch a happily married woman. She was always full of news about the other houses she worked for. That day, she went about her work rather quietly.

Gouri sat on the floor with a picture book in her lap.

"Lakshmi, why didn't Gouri go to school today?" I asked her, taking out ginger from the fridge for my tea.

"I couldn't go to school because Appa vomited on my bag," Gouri replied, before her mother could speak.

I observed; Lakshmi's face was swollen like a pumpkin and her one eye had turned black.

"And what happened to your face?" I asked Lakshmi.

"I fell down from the stairs," Lakshmi said without looking in my direction, her petite frame bent over the sink.

"Appa hit Amma with his belt," Gouri said innocently.

"Gouri! Keep quiet," Lakshmi raised her hand to hit her daughter.

"Lakshmi!" I raised my hand to stop her from hitting Gouri.

"Yes, he hit me but I am also no less. I bit him on the leg so hard that he will have to sit at home for a week. He is unable to walk, he is limping. I told him next time if he even touches me, I will kill him, I told him I will kill him." Lakshmi had blood in her eyes.

Lakshmi picked up the broomstick to go to the bedrooms.

"Useless fellow!" she mouthed, running her fingers over the bristles of the broom.

I stared at her back.

She had something which I didn't have. She had the courage to fight back.

I was not sure whether it was humanely possible to just shut my mind to the incident and, whether I would even be able to do that, but what else could I do? Lodging a police complaint against Navin was never an option. Vishal and his mother wouldn't have let me stay in their house if I would've even spoken about it. What would have happened to my marriage after that? Where would I go? The mourning period was now over. I had to find something to keep my mind occupied if I wanted to keep my sanity intact. Becoming an RJ in Bangalore had to wait until I could speak the local language fluently. Proficiency in Kannada was a prerequisite, and a language couldn't be learnt in a day. I thought of taking up a job but I didn't know how to hunt for one. In a fit of emotion, Vishal had given me his green signal; I wanted to quickly make use of it before he changed his mind. I took the newspaper and zeroed in on a few job vacancies, which I thought, fell within my reach. I didn't even have a proper resume; there was nothing to boast of. Qualification – BA incomplete (dropout), Skills –zero, Experience – zero.

Without even a bachelor's degree, the chances of finding a decent work were almost nil. Pursuing education for a few years and then looking for employment was out of the question. This incident had broken me completely; I pretended to be normal, but I had lost all urge to achieve anything in life. I didn't want to be famous, I wanted nothing; I only wanted someone who would love me without judging me.

Life was not a family melodrama; I realized when after three months and thirty phone calls, I was still sulking at home with nothing in my hand. I didn't get even an interview call. Every advertisement asked for experience.

I definitely had experience, but only in building castles in the air.

Harleen had influential people in her circle of friends. One phone call from any of the important people I had met in her parties was enough to get me some work, but my ego wouldn't allow me to approach her.

CHAPTER 23

I called Priya for advice. She was always there for me though I didn't help her when she needed me.

"Leela, it is difficult to get a decent job with your qualifications, and you don't even have any vocational skills." Priya was frank. "Why don't you look for some salesgirl kind of work, or some job in the lower cadre, like helpers in factories or housekeeping? They will make you slog like a donkey, but isn't it better than not doing anything at all? And most importantly you will get some work experience."

That was typical of Priya - she never minced words to tell the truth. I listened to her with gritted teeth. Was she my well-wisher, or what? It was demeaning to even think of housekeeping or helpers jobs, but the reality was that I was not capable of getting even those. I dreamt of becoming an RJ, but I was not worth even a C grade job, my inner voice mocked at me.

I ignored my inner voice and logged into Facebook to change my mood. I hadn't switched on my computer for more than a month.

There was not much action at Leela's profile except new pictures of Harleen's friends; I still called them Harleen's friends.

It was depressing to see their happy faces. Everyone was having fun in life except me or at least it seemed so. I logged out and logged into Elaa's profile. The messages and comments spilled out of my inbox. Elaa's friends were her real friends; at least they brought a smile to her lips. There were love notes, and messages that told me how much people missed Elaa.

There were four messages from Jai, my Facebook hero. I had almost forgotten about him.

You don't come on FB these days? Is everything okay with you?

I am in Delhi for some work for three days and then off to Bangalore and a few other places. Let us meet.

Msg me your cell number.

I was in Delhi; I thought you will see my msg and reply. I missed you. Wherever I looked, I saw your twinkling eyes.

Jai's messages perked me up. He had come down from Mumbai and wanted to meet me. He was also in Bangalore. He might be able to help me to get a job in Bangalore, may be as an RJ. Media guys are very resourceful. I was sure he would be of some use. But Leela wanted a job, and not Elaa. Jai knew only Elaa. I had to cook up a story without revealing my true identity.

I typed in the chat window.

Hi Jai, a friend of mine is looking for a job. She lives in Bangalore. Do you know someone there? I will appreciate if you can refer her somewhere. Any kind of job will do. She is in desperate need.

Regards Elaa

I kept my eyes glued to the chat window in anticipation of his reply. The chat window flashed exactly after three minutes and ten seconds. In response to my message, he had sent me a scanned copy of an advertisement.

Require freelance writers for writing articles on social issues. If you are well versed with country's social problems and have a flair for writing, send in your resume to New Times.

Ask your friend to email her resume to New Times. They will call her for the interview. I will put in a word.

What is your friend's name?

Mrs Leela Chopra, I replied without a thought.

That day I realized the benefits of social networking. I couldn't believe that my fake profile was helping me in getting a reference and that too for the job of a freelance writer in a popular English newspaper.

Instead of sending the resume by email, I decided to hand it over personally to the editor. I was curious to see the office where I was going to work.

"The editor is not in as yet, please have a seat," the receptionist at the office of New Times informed me. I occupied a vacant seat next to a young woman on the sofa and picked up the latest issue of Filmfare kept on a large teakwood table. Shah Rukh Khan, my favourite actor with his trademark dimpled smile, stared at me from the cover page. I flipped through its pages and kept it back. My mind was not on it. I was too anxious. I was eager to know what future had in store for me.

It was a posh office. Dull grey blinds on tall French windows, black leather sofas and two large side tables in teakwood with latest edition of New Times on every table - the office looked more like the lobby of a five-star hotel than a newspaper office. The wall behind the receptionist was painted in a natural mud colour. Soft music played in the background. I slipped my feet out from my *jutti* and relaxed. The shiny vitrified tiles below my feet felt refreshingly cold. I looked at my chipped toenails; the dead skin around my cuticles reminded me of a long overdue pedicure. I quickly wore my footwear and turned around to see if anyone was looking at my bare feet. I could see smartly dressed men and women moving around their cubicles. I looked dishevelled as compared to others.

I had waited for nearly an hour and still, there was no sign of the editor. I was tired of waiting. I got up from my seat to speak to the receptionist.

"Should I come some other day if it's going to be very late? This is regarding a job vacancy here."

"I will put you in touch with one of our correspondents, you can hand over your resume to him," she said after a thought. "Mr S. J. Venkataraman is one of our correspondents; he will be able to help you out," she said as she called S.J. Venkataraman on the intercom. "He will be here in a moment; please wait in the meeting room." She gestured me to go to a nearby room.

The ambience of the meeting room was as serene as the reception lobby, except for the whiff of tangy air freshener. The place smelt of success and professionalism. It was so exciting just to be there in that posh office, amongst the intellectuals. I wondered how it would be if I really got an opportunity to work here. I sat there and waited for Mr S. J. Venkataraman. Jai had not told me anything about this Venkataraman. Perhaps he had spoken only to the topmost person. I didn't know if I should give him Jai's reference. I kept my resume file on the table in front and picked up the newspaper.

"Hi, I am S. J. Venkataraman," a husky voice said from behind.

A hand stretched towards me for a handshake. I looked up from the newspaper in my lap. I raised my eyebrows and they didn't really move when I looked at the face in front. I blinked in disbelief. At that very moment, when I was fluttering my eyes stupidly and staring at the young man with my mouth open, I truly experienced the earth moving below my feet. I was so perplexed seeing the person that I forgot my name. Beads of sweat appeared on my forehead. Which was this place, why I was there? Darkness appeared in front of my eyes. I could see nothing except the face of my silent admirer glaring at me.

"Jai!" My mind said, but the words wouldn't leave my mouth.

Jai had been fooling me all these months; he didn't tell me that he was a journalist and lived in Bangalore. He said he worked for a TV channel in Mumbai. Is this person Jai, or Venkataraman? Multiple thoughts crossed my mind in quick succession.

When the hullabaloo inside my brain subsided and I gathered my senses together; I could not decide whether I should keep sitting or stand up. I tried to get up, but my butt was glued to the sofa.

In this perplexity, I forgot that I was the bigger fraudster. I had lied to him about everything: my marital status, my economic status, my education and my looks; at least his face was real. The expression on his face conveyed that he was equally shocked to see me. Did he think that Elaa and Leela were twin sisters, or two friends who happened to look alike?

"Miss Elaa Singh or Mrs Leela Chopra?" he asked sternly as he picked up my resume from the table, his eyes still on my face, perhaps trying to put together the pieces of the puzzle.

"MRS LEELA CHOPRA?" He read the name on my resume loudly.

I stood up.

"I asked you something. MISS Elaa Singh or MRS Leela Chopra? Who are you?" he asked again.

I shuddered.

I don't know any Elaa. I don't know what you are talking about, I wanted to say, but I was caught in my own web of lies. I was embarrassed; I was scared.

I was humiliated for making a fool of myself in front of a stranger. I wished the earth would open up and swallow me. I would have darted out of the door if Jai hadn't been standing right in the doorway.

"Are you Mrs Leela Chopra, or Miss Elaa?" He looked angry.

"Both," I opened my mouth at last, my eyes still downcast.

"No, you are not both. You look a lot like Elaa, but you cannot be Elaa." He looked confused and angry at the same time.

"Actually…" My voice trailed off.

He interrupted me. "So, all this time you were posing as another person? You fraud!"

Jai stood against the wall with arms folded across his chest. He wore a checked blue Arrow shirt and blue jeans. He tapped the wooden floor with his foot a few times before speaking.

"Why did you do this?" His body bent over the rectangular table as he spoke.

I was quiet. I could not make myself to look at him.

"A bored housewife trying to look pretty to trap young guys," he answered his own question. Seeing my teary eyes, he cut short his sentence.

I had lost my power of thinking logically. I didn't expect this fun game to end this way. For the next few seconds, the only sound in the room was the humming of air-conditioner.

He spoke after what seemed like forever. "Get out from here before I think of informing the police!"

I trembled.

"Get out, do you hear?" he shouted.

CHAPTER 24

After reaching home, I emptied a sachet of corn into the cooker and waited for it to pop. After sixty seconds, the corns started popping noisily. It sounded as if a lot of children were playing, dancing, yelling at each other playfully. The clattering sound was pleasing to my ears. I switched off the gas when the burnt smell hit my nostrils. Overcooking had turned the popcorn black. I opened the lid and emptied its contents into a big bowl. I perched on the sofa with the bowl in my lap. I picked one burnt corn and put it in my mouth. I liked the taste. I put the kernels in my mouth one by one while my mind played over the scene. *'A bored housewife trying to look pretty to trap young guys...'* Jai's words echoed in my mind. I was embarrassed all over again. When my nails scraped the bottom of the bowl, I realized I needed something to quench my thirst. I peeped into the refrigerator and found a half bottle of coke. I poured the liquid in a glass. It was insipid. The fizz from the bottle had escaped; quite like my own life.

I took a bar of chocolate and put a big piece in my mouth. I couldn't taste it; it seemed neither bitter, nor sweet. I wanted a mood lifter but when it didn't work, I reached for Vishal's stash and grabbed the first bottle that came to hand.

It was Johnnie Walker, a blended scotch whiskey. I was familiar with most of the names now. It was just that I still couldn't tell the difference between scotch, whiskey or any other type of alcohol; they all tasted the same to me. I poured some whisky in a glass and stood by the window. After taking a sip, I lit a cigarette and took a puff. I sucked the air and exhaled it slowly. With practice, I had learnt to smoke like Seema. I took another puff and then another and another; I was smoking like a habitual smoker.

I stood in front of the mirror with the glass and cigarette and, stared at my reflection. It looked hollow. I came closer and stared at it intensely. The reflection didn't change.

You are Leela, and you will always be Leela, whom no one loves. You can never be Elaa; boozing, smoking, wearing people's old clothes, enjoying on borrowed money, nothing can make you Elaa because YOU are not Elaa, my inner voice said.

I gulped down the last few drops of my drink and shut my inner voice. I logged into Facebook. Even after tossing down a large peg, I was in control of my senses. I opened and closed my fists in quick succession as I waited for the computer to boot.

I clicked on Jai's name.

I was welcomed with a message *'Do you know Jai? To see what he shares with friends, send him a friend request.'*

The message hit my face like a hard slap. He had knocked off my name from the list of his friends. Was I so bad that I was not worth even his virtual friend? Tears welled up in my eyes. Jai's angry face appeared in front of my eyes as I stared at the screen blankly.

I clicked on *'New Message.'*

My FB friend Jai,

I had forgotten that by changing one's appearance one cannot change one's destiny. It was foolish of me to even think that I could become Elaa just by changing my name and appearance. Elaa has reiterated my belief that if you are not destined to get something, you don't get it, no matter what... yes no matter what. Even my fake beautiful image was not worthy of anyone's affection.

Right from my childhood, I have never lived up to others' expectations. I am a dark complexioned and plain looking girl. If this is not enough, I am also a manglik. My older brother, Sanjay, looks exactly like my mother, with fair skin, light eyes. When I was two years old, my younger brother was born - a beautiful baby with chubby cheeks, just like my elder brother. I was the odd one out in the family.

"How come your daughter looks so different?" the relatives voiced. By 'different,' they meant dark and ugly.

I was only two years older than my younger brother but I was made to behave like his mother. He played in my mother's lap, whereas I was asked to fetch things for him. I never got to sit in my mother's lap after the birth of my younger brother.

At the time of my birth the Pandit ji had predicted that I was inauspicious. Wherever I would go, I would spread misery and doom to people around me. Pandit ji's prophecy proved true when my younger brother died of pneumonia. My parents wanted to give me up for adoption to a childless aunt because they didn't want my inauspicious shadow over my elder brother, but no one wanted me. My aunt and uncle later adopted a boy from an orphanage.

Though my parents never expressed this openly, I always felt that they didn't love me because they held me responsible for my brother's death.

My parents' conscious and sub-conscious actions led me to believe that I was unloved and unwanted. I was compared to Sanjay all the time. He got a new cycle but I didn't. I longed for a word of appreciation from my parents but I never got any.

My every action was condemned, I became reclusive and withdrew into a shell. 'Sanjay this, Sanjay that.' Why I can't be like Sanjay, why I can't do what Sanjay can do… I was sick of it. I started fearing Sanjay. I hated him. He hated me too. I studied hard, hoping for a single word of praise from my parents, but in return my father would say, "What is the need to study so much? Are you going to work?"

Every act of mine was criticized - how are you standing? How are you sitting? You don't even know this much? I started losing my confidence.

I was under constant surveillance. I loved my parents dearly and wanted to make them proud of me. I wanted to be a son to them. I wanted to become famous so they would be known as Leela's parents, and not Sanjay's. This is probably what gave birth to my obsession with becoming famous. My obsession with being an RJ, perhaps, has more to do with becoming famous than anything else.

I was in seventh heaven when Vishal liked me instantly. I thought my manglik days were over but the shadow of inauspiciousness continues even after marriage because I have failed here, too. Pandit ji was right; I can never make anyone happy, not even my husband.

Elaa was an offshoot of my desire to seek the admiration I was not fortunate enough to get from anyone. What Elaa gave me in six months; I have not got in twenty four years. Elaa got love and attention from strangers. Only I can understand this feeling of being unloved. I do regret that I fooled you but I am glad Elaa happened, because but for her, I would not have known what it is like to be loved and admired.

I assume you are still reading this message. I don't expect you to sympathize with me. I don't know why I am telling you all this but I feel like sharing this with you. I may not get another chance because our paths will never cross in life.

Goodbye,

Leela

Without a second thought, I clicked the send button. Such relief! I had had enough of dreaming. I wanted neither Jai nor Elaa anymore. I was sick of faking, I was sick of comparing myself to others all the time. My life had been a sham. I was sick of Facebook. Finally, I had figured out how to delete accounts. I deleted both my profiles. I had to make a new start all over again.

CHAPTER 25

It was naïve of me to even think of getting a job without a degree in hand, but I had neither the enthusiasm nor the patience to go back to fulltime education. Instead, I decided to do a short-term vocational course, which would partially equip me to stand on my own feet. Priya told me about a six-month course in Mass Communication. The institute was not a very reputed one, but the fee was nominal and they promised assistance in placements. Anyway, I didn't have much of a choice. Most of the well-known institutes not only had a very high cut off percentage, but they also refrained from admitting students with a gap in their education.

"What happened to your job hunting?" Vishal asked when I was serving him breakfast one Sunday morning.

Why did he have to ask? He knew very well that I hadn't found a job.

"Nothing has clicked so far," I replied slowly, placing another *aloo parantha* on his plate.

"So, ultimately, the fact has gone into your empty head that a dumb person like you cannot get a job! Didn't I tell you the same thing? But you never listen to me!" he said, giving me a look.

I didn't react to his comments. I had learnt to control my anger. The bruises on my arms were evidence of my arguments with him last week.

"Vishal, I have found out about a course in Mass Communication," I said. "It's a six month course and the fee is ONLY three thousand rupees per month. Six days, timings are from nine to three thirty. Can I join?" I parroted the rehearsed dialogue in a single breath.

He continued eating his breakfast in silence.

After finishing, he got up from the dining table and sat on the sofa with the supplement from the Sunday newspaper spread on his lap. I switched off the gas and followed him to the drawing room. His eyes were fixed on an article on page seven.

I stood in attention and looked at him in anticipation, as if he was about to announce some important result. Getting his consent was the most difficult hurdle, the challenges outside daunted me less.

"Please, can I join?" I begged.

"Okay," he said, head still buried in the newspaper.

I was not sure if I had heard right. I was expecting questions, counter questions, heated arguments and physical abuse over why I even thought of spending the money on the course, but nothing of that sort happened.

All goodies come with conditions in fine print. His consent, too, came with conditions attached to it. I was asked to do away with the services of my cleaning lady, Lakshmi, to save money towards my fees. It was not that he could not spend extra three thousand rupees a month, but, for him, anything spent on me alone was a waste of money. As a bargain, I also had to promise him that this course would not adversely impact my household responsibilities.

Despite all this, I was elated at the thought of getting an opportunity to study.

I daydream:

After I finish the course, I join New Times as a reporter. I am asked to attend a press conference addressed by the Chief Minister. The Chief Minister is a very manipulative and corrupt man. The journalists present there ask him only simple questions, not wanting to offend him by asking tough questions about his corrupt government, but I am bold. I ask him about all the scams that his cabinet is involved in, and he fumbles while answering. When I confront him for the wrongs his government has committed, he is speechless, but in his mind, lauds my courage to ask him tough questions. All the other journalists are looking at me in admiration. I am giving them a humble smile.

This course infused a new energy in me to finish the household chores before catching the eight o'clock bus for the institute situated on MG road. If I'd been asked to walk to the institute to save money on the bus, I would have done that also. I was so desperate for a breather that I was ready to do anything.

Breakfast was a hurried affair every day. I buttered some bread, much to the annoyance of Vishal, who relished an elaborate breakfast, complete with fresh juice, two stuffed *paranthas* and a bowl of papaya.

The evenings were spent cooking dinner, leaving me absolutely no time to do my assignments. In spite of my hectic schedule, I was enjoying every moment of my new life. It was like I was back in college again. The theory classes were conducted in the first half of the day, and the second half was dedicated to workshops and guest lectures. The theory sessions brought memories of my college days, when I sat on the first bench and captured the professor's every word in my notebook. Choosing clothes, matching accessories with the clothes (yes, I could find time for that), meeting new people, learning about the mad world of media, after-class gossip; it was a thrilling experience, which my early marriage had deprived me of. I still could not believe that Vishal had actually allowed me to enrol for this course.

CHAPTER 26

After class, the students would stay back to discuss their assignments, but I was always in a hurry to return home to do the household work. I was also the last one to submit my assignments, much after the due date. At home I worried about missed sessions and unfinished work sheets. In class, I thought about household work, unwashed vessels and the laundry. Despite my best efforts to balance, I was unable to cope with the pressures, but I didn't let the stress reflect on my familial responsibilities. People say behind every successful man there is a woman, but the reverse is equally true; a woman cannot succeed unless her man supports her.

The Institute of Journalism, the parent institute, regularly conducted workshops and seminars for its students. The sessions were also open to students from other colleges and media professionals. These workshops provided ample opportunities to meet people from related fields. That month's workshop was on script writing. The admission to these workshops was on first come first served basis. By the time I made up my mind to attend the workshop, all the seats were full, but I think my destiny was conspiring to push me towards this. My classmate Megha dropped out at the last moment due to an emergency at home, vacating the slot for me.

There were twenty-one participants for the workshop; sixteen men and five women. Most of them were working professionals or interns attached to various publications and media houses. Almost everyone was associated with writing in one way or the other. Mithun was in early thirties; he had attended the Film Appreciation workshop conducted by the institute earlier. He was keen on taking up a career in film scripting.

"I have written two books; after attending this workshop, I want to move to the next level, and write a script for a film," he said while introducing himself at the beginning of the session.

My heart started thumping hard when the first person in my row stood up to introduce himself.

"Does everyone have to introduce themselves?" I whispered to my neighbour, Neha.

I was not sure if I should say 'everyone have or has'.

"You should," Neha replied scornfully.

"I am Mrs. Leela Chopra, I am attending this workshop because there will be a lot to learn." I looked at my palm when I spoke; I had scribbled my introduction on it. I knew I would fumble while speaking in front of others; I might just say training instead of workshop.

"Leela, it's not a training, it's a workshop," the office clerk had corrected me, when I approached her for details about the script-writing workshop.

The first half of the opening session was dedicated to the theory. We were taught about concepts like the types of script writing, the difference between similar terminologies like story, script and dialogue writing. The speaker allotted the last fifteen minutes for interaction. Everyone was asking questions. I had a few questions, but couldn't muster enough courage to speak in front of others. I found my questions highly immature in comparison to those asked by others.

Next day, we were asked to write a script based on fictional characters.

"Your plot should be exactly one thousand and twenty words," Professor Sureena Khan instructed. "The next session is on the art of writing, by Mr. S.J. Venkataraman, a Correspondent from New Times. He will also evaluate your assignments and give you his feedback," she said before departing.

I froze in place. I had ended my virtual and real relationship with Jai by bidding him goodbye in the Facebook message, believing that our paths would never cross again, but destiny had willed it otherwise. Here I was again, about to go face - to - face with the person who had unmasked me. I just wanted to run away from there, but I had to face him. I regretted joining this workshop. I didn't want to ever see him again. The bittersweet memories of my online friendship with Jai started floating in my mind again.

I was brought back from my nightmarish world when I noticed a medium height figure in an olive green half-sleeve collared T-shirt, and black formal trousers entering the hall. Jai had grown a small French beard. I knew him. But still, it felt like he was a stranger.

I was sitting in the last row. I moved my chair a little to hide myself behind a tall woman sitting before me. I could partially see Jai's face, but he couldn't see mine.

There was a pin-drop silence in class when he spoke. Everyone listened with rapt attention. His grip over the subject was strong. The words flowed like water gushing out from a hot spring… no pauses, no ifs, no buts, no crutch words. He demonstrated lucidity of thought much beyond his years. I tried to guess his age; he was not more than thirty. He answered questions from students with immense maturity, reflecting his rich experience in writing and journalism. Every word from his mouth transported the audience to a different world. Then the inevitable happened. The tall woman in front of me moved her chair to the left, exposing me to the person who had threatened to hand me over to the police. There was no way I could escape this. My heart started pounding hard in anticipation of something unpleasant. Jai paused for a second and raised his eyebrows when his eyes spotted me. From the surprised look on his face, I could tell that he, too, was not prepared for this chance meeting, but he quickly calmed down his surprised look and continued with his interactive session as if he had not recognized me.

"Where is Hamas? Why has Israel been in the news for so many years?" Jai questioned the students. Three students raised their hands to answer.

"How about the rest of the students?" he questioned. With the wave of his hand, he asked those three students to keep their hands down and continued with his lecture. "While writing a script it is very important that you are well informed about the location of the scene. You should be able to feel the character, visualize what he eats, what he dreams, whether he is thin or fat, study even small incidents. In brief, live the life of that character to inject life into it."

He paused, waiting for the students to digest what he had said.

"Once you have read and thought about all that, only then pick up your pen and paper to write, and not before that."

"Sir, do we have to write on paper first? Can't we type into the computer directly?" Divya asked, eliciting roar of laughter from the entire class.

Jai was silent for a moment, perhaps offended at being interrupted; he then joined the class' laughter. He had a full-throated laugh. He tossed back his head slightly as he laughed; his eyes twinkled like the eyes of a cat in dark. I glanced at Neha, who was staring at him with her hands clasped under her chin. A smile played on her lips as she looked at Jai with admiration.

"What a sexy laugh!" Neha mumbled, winking at me.

Jai stopped abruptly when he caught me gawking at him, my eyes blinking a wee bit too late. Our eyes met and remained locked for more than a second. He was not handsome in the conventional sense but there was a kind of aura about him. I was reminded of his Facebook messages. He was my silent admirer. Irrespective of what had transpired between us in his office, I admitted, I still had a soft corner for him. He was the only one in my life who had words of praise for me; even if it was a wrong number, the number was mine.

"I can't listen to all your scripts because we don't have the time. Give your scripts to me. I will go through them and get back to you on your strengths and areas that need improvement," Jai announced to the class.

The students got up to hand their sheets over to Jai. Sitting on the last bench, I reread my script, but didn't budge from my seat.

I folded my papers and kept them in my handbag. I didn't want to become the laughing stock of the class by exhibiting my amateur writing skills in front of professional writers.

"Has everyone submitted their scripts?" Jai asked the class.

"Yes," the entire class chorused, including me.

CHAPTER 27

When I woke up in the morning, Vishal had already left for work. I looked at my watch with groggy eyes. It was already nine a.m. I had missed the first lecture. My body ached from the last night's beatings. Yesterday, Vishal had hit me badly on my back. How I wished I were capable enough to fend for myself and escape from this living hell! I wanted to go back to sleep but I forced myself to get out of the bed. Instead of crying in bed the whole day, it was better to go out to breathe some fresh air. My cheek was still red from the slap Vishal had given me last night, but I no longer gave a damn about what people would say about my red cheek. I jumped out of the bed to get ready. I grabbed the first salwar kameez set that fell from the cupboard and darted to the bathroom. There was no time to eat breakfast. I gulped down a glass of chilled water and left. When I reached the bus stop, the bus was right there, as if waiting for me. At least something good was happening today.

I was just in time for the second lecture. I was unable to concentrate on the teacher's words in the class. I hadn't eaten anything since last night. I let out a yawn, thinking of the messy kitchen and unmade beds. After the classes got over, I rushed to the bus stop. There was no bus in sight even after waiting for half an hour. I was drained of all my energy. I signalled a few passing by autos to stop, but in vain. I had to walk to the auto stand on the opposite side of the road. With a notebook under my arm and the handbag swinging from the other shoulder, I waited for the pedestrian signal to turn green. As the signal changed, the pedestrians on both sides of the road started surging towards the other side, almost running into people coming from the opposite direction.

"Hi," I heard someone call me.

I turned my face towards the direction of the voice. All of a sudden, my feet stopped moving as if they were chained to the spot. I forgot the direction in which I was going. This couldn't be true. Was it really a coincidence, or a bigger strategy by God?

I didn't expect to see Jai ever again, and here I was meeting him on a pedestrian crossing in the middle of heavy traffic. I stood there fluttering my eyelashes like a bird flapping its wings to fly. The traffic signal had turned green by then and the traffic had started crawling, resulting in a frenzy of honking.

He clutched my wrist and pulled me to the other side of the road.

"You are back to the place from where you started," Jai said, handing me the notebook that had fallen on the road, his hand still encircling my wrist lightly.

He was staring at my bruised cheek.

I guessed that he would figure out what caused the red patch on my skin.

"Meet my colleague Rohit, and Rohit, she is Leela - Leela Chopra," he said, introducing me to the man standing next to him.

I was flattered, he remembered my full name.

"We are going for coffee. You know, the coffee in the office is horrible. Why don't you also join us, if you are free?" Jai asked.

I looked at him.

His eyes spoke more than words. There was something in the way he asked me that made it impossible for me to refuse. I nodded and started walking with them. I did not know what to call him - Raman, Venkat, Venkataraman or Jai. For me, he was Jai and I was curious to know the mystery behind his fake identity on Facebook. We walked towards the coffee house silently. The air was thick with anxiety. I noticed he was not very tall, may be a few inches shorter than Vishal.

As we walked together on the pavement, Jai made small conversation while Rohit was on phone all the time.

"What do you like most about Bangalore?" Jai asked me, as we sat across from each other in a tiny south Indian eatery.

"Everything," I replied.

Rohit was sitting at the edge of the table with the phone stuck to his ear; at times talking on two phones simultaneously with a phone glued to each ear.

"What brings a Punjabi *Kudi* to the South, two thousand kilometres away from her home town?" Rohit asked after finishing his call.

"But how do you know I am from Punjab?" I asked innocently.

"Because you speak English in Punjabi," Rohit said, as he exchanged a half smile with Jai.

Something in my heart tore. Not because I speak English with a Punjabi accent, but because Rohit knew something about me. Had Jai told him about my fake identity and the sob story I wrote to him?

"Come on, Rohit." Jai laughed. "Hey Leela, don't pay any attention to Rohit, he is simply pulling your leg," Jai explained. "It is actually because of the way you dress - short kurtis, loose salwar, matching bangles and Punjabi *jutti* - anyone can tell you are not from the South," Jai said plainly, as if reading the news. Saying this, he exchanged another smile with Rohit.

There was a strange silence between Jai and me.

To my relief, Jai broke the silence. "Have you read our Society page? Why don't you write for it? Write about interesting people in the city. To start with, why don't you interview your friend, Priya, and write about how, being a woman, she copes with the erratic life of a pilot," he said, looking into my eyes and occasionally at my bruised cheek.

During one of our daily Facebook chats, I had told him about Priya to impress him about my extensive social circle.

"Write in simple but forceful language and always remember to…" He continued his speech.

I found myself looking at him intensely, pretending to hang on his every word. I just cannot stop staring at your face, Jai. You are perfect in every aspect- what was the need to fake it? I wanted to ask him so badly, but I didn't.

He had straight, neatly cut hair; sharp, intelligent eyes and distant eyebrows. I couldn't make out whether his eyes were black or brown; it had a tinge of both the shades, but more of brown. His face was broad, but also on longish side, and not moon shaped like Vishal's. Dusky complexion not dark like mine, long sharp nose, and light brown fully curved lips added to his boyish charm. A soft dimple showed on his right cheek when he stretched his lips into a smile.

I quickly turned my face away when Jai paused in the middle of a sentence; he had caught me observing his facial expressions.

"Hello, where are you?" he waved his fingers in front of my nose to bring me back.

Embarrassed, I suddenly got up.

"I should leave now, I am getting late," I said. Even before I knew what I was saying, I had reached the door of the coffee shop. From the corner of my eyes, I saw him looking at me through the large glass window while I walked shyly on the footpath. His face was expressionless; the breeze blew, making my hair fly back and forth on my face. I walked some distance, only to realize that I was walking in the opposite direction. I stopped, giggled and said to myself, it wasn't me who was walking in the wrong direction, it was my life. I couldn't get my mind off Jai. It was my first brush with infatuation.

I hailed an auto and jumped in. Instead of taking a U-turn, the auto driver continued to drive straight.

I asked him, "Bhaiya, aren't we going in the opposite direction? Why are you going this way?"

To which he replied, "No madam, we are going in the right direction, this is a one way."

Life indeed was a one way.

CHAPTER 28

I had laughed it off when Jai suggested writing for the Women's section of New Times, but the idea remained in my mind. I had never written anything longer than an email or a letter and, of course, that one page for the script-writing workshop. I had never been interested in writing, but I was studying Mass Communication with the intention of joining a related field, so what was the harm in trying? I picked up the pen to write, but my mind was blank. I flipped through a few old magazines for ideas. Nothing appealed to me; all the topics there were done to death.

I picked up the phone to call Priya for some suggestions.

"Great! So you are thinking of becoming a writer?" Priya asked.

"*Naa re,* just passing my time. I am studying Mass Communication, so it helps to improve my writing skills," I clarified. I didn't want to tell her that Jai was the reason I was taking this up, not my course.

"Why don't you write about single women, single mothers or something similar," Priya suggested. "There are not many articles on this subject."

Priya seemed contented in her own small world, but I always thought she was unhappy because she was not settled in the conventional sense of the word - marriage, husband, children, in-laws, but does marriage bring happiness?

"Priya, tell me about yourself. Do you think you are lonely because...?" I left the question hanging. I cut short of saying 'single,' she might find it offensive.

"Come on, Leela! The times have changed. Today's woman doesn't need a husband to be happy. In fact, she doesn't need a husband even to become a mother. I am not lonely, I have my work, my house, and my daughter," she said. "And I love my independence, I don't want to get tied up in a relationship," she added.

"Oh yes, yes."

"Leela, it's nice that you are happily married, but everyone is not as lucky as you," Priya said.

Priya had opened my wounds. She wouldn't have said this if she knew what really happened inside the four walls of my house. I never felt close enough to Priya to discuss my personal life with her. There are some things in life, which you cannot discuss with everyone. I had an image to maintain in front of Priya and Harleen. How could I shatter that?

I dropped the idea of writing; I knew I wouldn't be able to write, it was not in me.

"So what are you writing about?" A text message flashed across my screen one morning. I wondered who had sent this message to me.

"Who is this?"

"Your ex FB friend!"

"How do you have my number?"

"I have your resume, you forgot!" Jai messaged.

"So what are you writing on?" he asked again.

"I am writing about single women, almost done," I lied.

"Great, send it to me quickly."

Like always, I was caught in my own web of lies. Now I had to write something to convince him that I was not a total dud. I compiled opinions of some of the women in my building and churned out a seven hundred word article. I wanted to get it reviewed by someone before sending it to make sure that it made sense. Of all the people I knew, I trusted Priya's opinion the most.

"Nice, send it," Priya responded within an hour.

Priya was neither a writer nor an editor, but her English was good. She was a modern woman, capable of evaluating my article.

After two days, I received an email from New Times.

Dear Leela,

Your piece requires minor editing. I have forwarded it to our Women's section for consideration. Meanwhile, keep writing.

Cheers,

SJ

I was elated. I read his email for the seventh time. An email from Jai was like a dose of adrenalin. Did he like my article? Was it really good?

I daydream:

I am writing articles regularly for reputed publications. In the 'Readers Speak' column, many readers compliment me on my writing skills and off beat thoughts. Not everyone agrees with what I write, but they all want my opinion on the matter anyway. The editor is happy with the wonderful response; he decides to give me a weekly column. Readers look forward to the Saturday edition of the paper to read my column. The publication gives me one thousand rupees per column. Vishal is telling his boss about me, 'Sir, my wife writes for the newspapers.' Everyone knows me. 'That Leela Chopra, who writes for New Times.' That's how people identify me.

I listed out a few topics. I was already thinking of the next article. However, patience is the virtue of the wise; I decided to wait until my first piece was published.

"Nice article in the paper, Leela!" an SMS from Harleen read one Saturday morning.

The paperboy had not brought the newspaper that day. I sprinted to Sapna's apartment to get the newspaper.

"Sapna! Sapna! Has the paperboy delivered the paper today? Mine hasn't come yet. My article has come in today's paper," I blabbered as I walked into her apartment. I leapt at the newspaper kept on the centre table.

I opened the newspaper to find an article with my by–line. *'Single but Happy' by Leela Chopra.* My by-line shone on the third page of the weekly supplement. I stared at the paper. This was the first time my name had been published in the paper. Nothing but my by-line was visible to me.

By Leela Chopra. I read my name aloud. A smile of pride played on my lips.

"Oh ya, nice article, I saw it today morning, I was about to call to congratulate you," Sapna complimented me.

"Really, you liked it? I have written it," I said hopefully.

Before I could think of informing Priya, she called me. She had read my article. "Good one, keep it up." Priya sounded genuinely happy at my small achievement.

"Do you write articles? I saw your name in the paper today, I thought must be you because you are studying Mass Communication," an elderly woman from the opposite block asked me while I was returning from Sapna's apartment with newspaper in tow.

"Yes, Aunty, I have written it." I beamed from ear to ear.

I was elated. I had become a kind of mini celebrity in the building. I came home and called my parents. I wanted my father to be the first one to know in my family. I wanted him to pat me on my back and say – "Well done beta, I am proud of you." In all my life, I could not recall a single moment when my parents had complimented me. No one picked up the phone. Daddy ji didn't have a cell phone.

I called Sanjay.

"Really? Your article is published in an English newspaper? You must have copied it from somewhere," Sanjay mocked.

There was no need to call Vishal. Expecting a word of praise from him was asking too much.

I made myself a cup of lemon tea and perched on the sofa with the newspaper in hand.

'By Leela Chopra... ' I read it aloud. This was a baby step in my journey to fame. My expression changed as I read the first paragraph, then the second, then the third and the entire article.

The piece looked completely different from the original one. The sentences were crisp. The grammar had been improved. The words were catchy; some of them unfamiliar to me. It was punctuated correctly. There were no superfluous words. Words came alive as my eyes scanned the paper. The basic idea, that a single woman need not always be lonely, was retained, but it was presented in a very appealing way. I noticed even the caption had been changed. It looked like a masterpiece to me. Nothing was mine except the by-line. My enthusiasm burst like a pierced balloon. I didn't deserve the adulation.

I was angry for making a fool of myself once again in front of Jai. He had rewritten the article for me and given me the credit. I felt small; I felt insulted. I felt incapable.

CHAPTER 29

A week later, my mobile buzzed, when the class was working on writing catchy captions. My eyes drifted from the notebook to the cell phone. I had been trying to write some good captions for the six news stories given to us, but nothing impressive had struck so far.

"Coffee?" Jai had messaged.

I was so engrossed in the gory news stories that it took me a few seconds to register that Jai was inviting me for coffee.

"@ 3.45 pm 2day," my cell buzzed again when I didn't respond to his message for fifteen minutes. It was not that I was acting pricey because a guy had invited me for coffee, but my mind was working overtime to analyse why he had asked me out.

Why ME?

Should I go? Shouldn't I? I asked myself.

After all, it was just a coffee. A coffee, nothing more than that!

"I am busy," I wanted to type but instead I typed, *"Where?"*

"Pedestrian crossing!!!" he replied within a flash.

I smiled. My anger vanished and a strange tender feeling for Jai erupted from nowhere.

This was my first date, if meeting someone for coffee in a crowded café is called a date. This would have been a heady feeling if I were an unmarried woman. I was excited, not because this was the first time a man had asked me out, but because there was someone in the entire world who thought of spending an hour of his time with me, just with ME. I didn't know whether I was nervous or excited, may be both. Should I shake hands with him or just say hi? Would handshake signal drooling over him, or was that the way the big city girls do?

I had seen the girls in my class shake hands with men while greeting them. What was the harm in shaking hands? After much deliberation, I decided I would not shake hands with him, even if he brought his hand forward.

I walked towards the cafe. From a distance, I spotted Jai outside the café. With one hand in his pocket, another holding the phone to his ear, Jai looked suave in a slate grey formal shirt and jeans. He looked so different from the rest of the men around him; or was it my tenderness for him that made me see him that way?

A married woman going on a date with a stranger..., my inner voice chastised me.

It's not a date, I'm just meeting him for coffee, I argued with myself meekly.

Jai is neither your colleague, nor your classmate, and definitely not your friend. Why are you going out with him? My inner voice almost shouted, making me feel guilty of projecting myself as easily available. I shouldn't have come. I was in half a mind to return, but before I could think of going back, Jai had seen me. He waved at me as he kept the phone back in his shirt pocket. I felt a sudden rush of blood to my head when our eyes met.

"Hi." I smiled, stretching my hand for a handshake even before he could do so.

"Hi." He smiled back, reciprocating with a quick handshake.

We occupied a table right in the centre, the only vacant table in the cafe.

"What would you like to have?" Jai asked me, as the waiter stood by for the order.

Once, Harleen had ordered a Green apple soda for herself when we had gone out to a cafe. I didn't order one for myself then because I didn't want to sound like I was copying her. The tall glass had appeared classy in her manicured hands.

"One Green apple soda," I said.

"Madam, Green apple soda is not available," the waiter replied.

"Okay, black coffee then," I said.

"Something to eat?" Jai asked me, with his eyes on the menu card.

"No, I am not hungry," I lied. A chocolate pastry would have been great, but I didn't want to be perceived as a glutton, and eating chocolate pastry is so unfeminine. No figure conscious woman eats pastry in public, and that too chocolate pastry. The modern women ate only diet food and black sugarless coffee in public.

"Two coffees and two chocolate pastries please," Jai told the waiter.

Was he a mind reader? How did he know that I wanted to have a chocolate pastry?

"What do you generally like to drink - scotch, wine, beer or something else?" I asked to conceal the surprised look on my face. I wanted to sound well informed about drinks on my so called first date.

"I don't drink," he replied flatly.

I was in for a surprise again. In my opinion, all journalists were drunkards, looking for opportunities to enjoy free liquor. That was what I had heard from Neha and a few of my other classmates.

"Oh! So you are a teetotaller."

"Not even a teetotaller, I don't drink tea, I take only coffee."

He smiled, and I smiled, too. His terrific sense of humour was addictive.

"My full name is Srinivasa Jaishankar Venkataraman, but everyone calls me S.J.," Jai said. "Jai is a short form of my middle name but except you no one calls me by this name," he added calming my curiosity about his Facebook name. He was twenty-nine years old. New Times was his fourth job. He confessed that in spite of doing extremely well in his profession, journalism didn't interest him. He still hadn't figured out what he wanted from life. By his own admission, he lacked focus, and was very moody and restless by nature. Giving out fake details on Facebook was just a way of relieving his boredom. Tamilian by origin, Jai was brought up in Chennai. Both his parents were journalists. As a child, his addiction for computers made him opt for Computer Science in college, but after three semesters in engineering, he realized he would do anything in life, but not engineering. Despite pressure from his family, he dropped out. He got into journalism because he said writing was in his genes.

"So everything about you in Facebook is false?" I asked. Frankly, I was more concerned whether he had a girlfriend as he had mentioned, but I couldn't ask him such a personal question.

"Except for my girlfriend, everything else was false. I was in a relationship at that time, but we broke up," he explained.

I raised my eyebrows again at the strange telepathy we shared.

His honest confession took the guilt out of me that I was meeting someone's boyfriend though it was not that I had any romantic inclinations towards him. For my own convenience, I simply forgot that even though he was unattached and single, I was very much married.

Why he had invited me for coffee? Was he attracted towards me? Did he find me interesting? Or was it just because he had nothing else to do? My head was a whirlpool of thoughts. It was only later in life I realized that everything in life cannot follow a cause and effect pattern, everything need not have a reason.

After a few meetings, my initial inhibitions had disappeared, and I didn't feel that it was immoral to just meet a guy and talk to him. Jai had a casual, easygoing attitude. I found myself opening up to him. My institute was very close to his office. We met whenever he texted me. We chatted over endless cups of coffee- always the same café, same time and the same table, right in the centre of the cafe. It was interesting to listen to him.

"Frankly, in all my life, I haven't met anyone who talks candidly about becoming famous. It's so refreshing," he said. "You are so simple and nice."

I could only smile at it. I didn't know how to handle the compliment.

"How about meeting for coffee on Friday?" he suggested when we got up to leave, and I, like an attention starved woman, blurted 'Sure.'

Before leaving, he gave me a book.

"It is written by a friend of mine," he said. "It's my personal copy; you can read it at leisure, and return it later, no hurry."

There was something about Jai that pulled me towards him; he was so genuine. The most desired gift of love is not diamonds, it is undivided attention. He was giving me something which I had craved all my life. He told me about the Facebook message I had sent him but didn't ask me anything else about my personal life. It was like he understood everything even without my telling him.

CHAPTER 30

I decided to give our Friday coffee meeting a miss due to a cigarette burn that Vishal gave me on my hand. It seemed strange how I had submitted myself to all the torture. It was like daily chores. Like doing vessels or washing clothes, getting beaten up and burned had become a part of my life. My tolerance was bursting at its seams, but I couldn't muster enough courage to resist the physical blows lashed on me every other day. I was still the same old Leela who was always scared of her husband. I didn't even have the guts to think about divorcing him. My parents' hopeful faces would come in front of my eyes whenever the thought of leaving Vishal entered my mind. The loss of a child, a married son who was not capable of earning a single penny-my parents had faced many setbacks in life; my marriage into a 'respectable family' had given them some happiness at least. Would I want to snatch that from them? How could I be so selfish and break their illusion by announcing that I had a troubled marriage.

I kept my promise to Jai and met him for coffee after a week when my burn mark had faded a bit. My heart missed a beat when I looked at him. He looked so handsome in a chocolate brown T-shirt. As we sat across from each other in the restaurant, I realized the burn mark on my hand was still clearly visible when I saw Jai's gaze shifting from my eyes to my hand occasionally.

"What happened on your hand?" he asked.

"Oh, it's nothing, drops of oil spilled on my hands while frying," I lied, tucking my hand under the table.

I sounded so confident, as if this was really an accident in the kitchen. I started talking about my batchmates, the class in the morning. I didn't know what I was talking about, I was just blabbering, my mind was thinking about the cigarette marks, about our fight last night, about my incapability and helplessness to get out of the living hell that was my house.

While talking I rested my arms on the table, and he put his hand on mine. I first looked at him, and then at his hand kept above mine. I didn't make any effort to slip my hand from his grasp. There were no romantic overtones in his touch. It was purely a friendly gesture.

I blinked back a tear, to prevent it from falling on his hand.

"Leela, it's your life, do what you think is right. It is up to you how you decide to live it," Jai said as we got up to leave.

I didn't reply. My heart was heavy with emotions. That day was the last day of my course, and Jai was taking a two-week break from work. He was going to one Yoga centre for a two-week meditation course.

"I want to think about what I want to do in life," he said.

I had no idea if we would be able to meet so frequently after the completion of my course.

We walked together towards our respective destinations; I, to the auto stand, and he, to his office. As usual, Jai was on phone with one of the reporters from his office. Evenings were busy times for journalists, and mornings were not possible for me, so we had stuck to the 3.45 p.m. coffee break, until the end of my course. I walked along silently, matching my steps with his, and not the two steps behind I was used to with Vishal.

Now and then he looked at me, probably to make sure I was still walking with him. We reached the same pedestrian crossing where I had met him six months ago. There was mad traffic on the road. The traffic lights at the signal were not working. As we stepped onto the road, a car zipped past us, and we pulled back. We moved ahead again to cross, but speeding vehicles pushed us back. When the traffic slowed down a bit for a few seconds, we tried to cross the road. We were half way through when the approaching vehicles forced us to jump on the median. I was getting restless. I didn't want to be seen in the middle of the road with a guy. What if any of Vishal's colleagues saw me and informed him! Blood drained from my face as I thought of the calamity that might befall me if that ever happened.

We had to cross the road, and there was no way traffic was going to stop for us. So, again we stepped on the road. With his mobile still stuck to his left ear, as we manoeuvred our way through the speeding vehicles, his arm stretched in front of me to shield me from the speeding vehicles.

I blushed when the hair on his arm tickled my face. I clutched his arm, as the zipping traffic blew my hair across my face. I looked at him; he was engrossed in the conversation with Rohit, discussing the front-page news for tomorrow. Unknowingly he had stretched a hand of protection towards me. Unknowingly I, too, had hung on to his protective arm.

It took us almost ten minutes to cross the road. Something happened in those ten minutes; those ten minutes changed my life.

Putting both his arms around my shoulders, he gave me a quick hug. Encompassed in his protective hug, all the worries in the world seemed trivial to me. In those microseconds, when I was close to his body, I felt relieved, I felt as if I was not alone.

'The Quarter Circle' by Monashree. I took out the book that Jai had given me to read.

"I am thankful to my friend S.J. Venkataraman, who took time off from his extremely busy schedule to review my book. Without him, this book wouldn't have seen the light of the day." Monashree had mentioned on the acknowledgement page.

Subconsciously I ran my fingers over Jai's name. Every word, every sentence, every page, brought me closer to him. After a few sentences, I paused to imagine what Jai would have thought when he read that page. Did he smile after reading this, I wondered after reading something funny. I visualized him reading the book lying on the bed in a reclining posture just the way Vishal did, his shorts revealing his hairy legs.

"I always see you with this fat book. Haven't you finished it yet?" Vishal asked me one day.

"Oh, I finished it long back, I'm reading it for the fifth time," I replied dreamily.

"Fifth time? Are you crazy?"

I knew I had gone crazy. I felt like a lovelorn teenager. My day started and ended with thoughts of Jai. Every time we met, sparks flew and my heart fluttered with desperate anticipation. I recalled my first meeting with Jai in his office. At that time, I didn't know that one day this man would become the focal point of my life. I had a huge crush on him. I loved when my heart flip-flopped in my chest on seeing his name flash across my mobile screen. He was omnipresent, like an invisible man listening to me, smiling with me. I allowed myself to be swayed by these feelings. It was such a beautiful feeling to be in love. Whether it was the storm before the lull, or lull before the storm, I didn't understand. All I wanted was to hear his deep voice. I knew I was falling in love with him. Love or infatuation, I didn't know, neither did I want to know. He meant the world to me. I didn't know what he thought of me; did he know I was smitten by him? Did he feel something for me? Perhaps yes, otherwise why should he go for coffee with me or even send me SMSes. I adored my fantasy world with Jai where both of us were in love with each other. Life had changed for me. I felt desired.

You are falling into a trap, and not in love, my inner voice admonished me. Get up before you fall. He will ruin you emotionally, my inner voice preached.

Like always, I didn't listen to my inner voice. Just once in life I wanted to listen to my heart. Just once, I wanted to know how it felt to be in love.

CHAPTER 31

After my course ended, I applied for a job at a few places but nothing had materialized so far. My life was back to cooking, eating, sleeping, taking evening walks, and watching TV. I hadn't spoken to Jai for almost a month. Jai had promised to call me after he returned from the Yoga centre, but he hadn't.

I always kept my cell phone next to me in anticipation of his phone call. I hadn't seen any of his articles in New Times for a long time. I had started maintaining a file of his articles. By now I was so familiar with his style of writing that even if there was no by - line I could tell if the piece was written by him. The article always ended with a punch. It invariably ended with a thought provoking question.

I picked up the phone to call him, but gave up the thought. He was probably in a meeting or he might have gone to meet his parents in Chennai.

At last, I gave in to my desperation and called him, but the number didn't get through. I tried a couple of times but something seemed to be wrong with the network.

I called his office.

"He is not with New Times any longer," the operator informed me.

Jai had resigned, and hadn't even bothered to tell me.

"Can you put me across to Rohit, or someone who knows where he is working now?"

"At this time no one is around, all the reporters have gone on their beats. Please call after five; everyone will be here then," the operator said.

I called again at five, but the number was busy. Another time when I called, the operator put me on hold. I hung up when no one came on the line for five long minutes.

He might have lost his mobile, and didn't have my number. I thought of all possible excuses which could prevent Jai from contacting me.

One afternoon, when I had just laid down for a nap, my cell phone buzzed. I pressed the answer button with my eyes closed.

"Hey Leela!" I heard a familiar voice at the other end.

I got up with a start. It was as if someone had injected life into a dead body. This was Jai, my Jai. I was too happy to utter a word. Jai's baritone uplifted my spirits. I had a new energy. He always called when I least expected it. I felt a deep urge to throw my arms around him and tell him how much I loved him. There was not a single moment in all these months when I didn't think of him.

"It's been three months since you called," I said. 'And twenty days' I wanted to add. I didn't let my voice reveal that my life revolved around him.

"I was really very busy," he said plainly.

"Jai, I love you," I blurted.

He was taken aback, perhaps more by the passion in my tone, than my words. There was silence. I thought he had disconnected the line.

What he must be thinking about me, I am a married woman and making advances towards him, I so wished I could take my words back.

"So how is everything else with you?" Jai asked changing the topic.

I was too numb to answer him.

Jai was in New York on an eighteen-month assignment with a private TV channel. I didn't want to waste time talking about myself. I just wanted to hear his voice, and feel his presence on the other side. He talked about his new job, his life in New York, the people, the nightlife, the lively city. He sounded very indifferent. There was no warmth in his voice.

"Okay, all the best. Maybe our paths will cross in the future sometime," he said, leaving me to wonder what he meant. Did he mean we would meet only if our paths cross by chance? What if they don't?

I was heartbroken. All doors in life seemed closed to me. I heard glass break somewhere. The sound was deafening. I visualized glass pieces strewn all over the floor. Minuscule pieces of glass pierced my skin when I tried to take a step. I was scared to keep my feet on the ground again. I wished he hadn't called. I was so happy in my dream world. I could have lived my entire life in the illusion that there was someone in this world who loved me. Why did he call and shatter my dream? He didn't love me. He left for the US and he didn't call even once to inform me. Didn't I mean anything to him? I sobbed uncontrollably until I had no more tears.

Jai was like a mirage. He disappeared when I thought I had inched closer to him. I had been living in an illusionary world with him, in which he was madly in love with me. An impersonal phone call from Jai had destroyed my dreamy world.

Jai's call transported me back to my aimless life. Earlier I had a mission to accomplish, an agenda for the day, a purpose in life. I had to bring myself up to look into his eyes and say "Hey Jai, I am not less than anyone."

I had lost all reason to live. Whom do I live for now, I asked myself. Suddenly, I felt detached from everything around me - my aspirations, my dreams, nothing mattered if Jai was not with me.

CHAPTER 32

One night the doorbell rang. I immediately woke up. Switching on the bedside lamp, I squinted at the wall clock. It was two a.m. The bell rang again. I dragged myself out of the bed and opened the door. I was surprised to see my cleaning lady Lakshmi at the door. She had started working in our house again after I finished the Mass Communication course.

Before I could think why she had come at that unearthly hour, she fell at my feet.

"Amma, please let Gouri stay in your house for one night. Damodar, my husband is selling Gouri to that man, Amma! Amma! Please help me." Lakshmi was hysterical, her sobs breaking the peace of the night.

Dressed in a long skirt and loose blouse, Gouri was hiding behind her mother. She came in front, looking at me with pleading eyes. Gouri wore a terrified expression on her face. She was holding a red haired doll which I had given her on her birthday. I had even sewn a red dress for the doll with white polka dots. Gouri was very fond of this toy.

"Who is there?" Vishal called from the bed.

"No one," I replied. "I mean, Lakshmi."

I peeped down. The corridor on our floor overlooked the main gate of the building. A man stood near the main gate, a bottle in his hand. He was shouting at the top of his voice, hurling abuses in Kannada. It was obvious he was inebriated.

"What is this maid servant doing here at night?" Vishal had come to the door by then.

"Vishal, we've got to help her," I said, quickly narrating everything.

"Have you gone crazy? Get them out of here immediately." He tried to force the door shut.

"Amma, please!" Lakshmi stood in the doorway, preventing Vishal from closing it. "If not in your house, let her stay outside in the corridor," Lakshmi pleaded.

"Vishal, please don't do this." I held the door open with my hand.

I had never seen Lakshmi crying. She didn't cry when her husband hit her. Today, she was sobbing.

"Vishal, let them stay here for the night. Her husband is selling her daughter. He is so drunk, he can do anything," I beseeched. "They will go home in the morning."

Lakshmi became hopeful when she saw me pleading her case.

"Amma, take me to the police station, I will lodge a complaint against my husband."

"I think that's the least we can do," I suggested nodding my head.

"You are a fool! If she is so dear to you, then you also go with her. I don't run a guest house," Vishal said, pointing his finger towards the door. “I don't want to get involved with the police. And stop behaving like her guardian.” He pulled me inside and shut the door.

Vishal went into the bedroom.

“Come and sleep now,” he called from the bedroom.

I came to the bed reluctantly, but sleep was miles away. My heart went out to Lakshmi, but I was too scared of my husband to disobey him. I closed my eyes and tried to sleep. I pictured Gouri being dragged to a brothel, men pouncing on her tender body. Vishal had turned his face to the other side. On hearing him snore, I tiptoed to the living room, finding my way in the dark, and looked down from the window. Damodar was dragging Lakshmi by her hair, his other hand holding a bottle of cheap liquor. He was hurling abuses. Gouri was sobbing and trailing behind them. In between sobs, she looked up at the window. The little girl could not fathom what was in store for her. My eyes followed them until I could not see them anymore.

“Lakshmi has not come for work for the past three days. I think we should have helped her that day,” I told Vishal as I rolled *paranthas* for breakfast on a Sunday morning.

“Why should you feel guilty, their life is like that. Why is she putting up with an alcoholic husband?” he said, turning his head in my direction. “One day, they will be at each other's throats, and next day they will produce a baby. You unnecessarily get carried away by their polite words.”

Lakshmi's life was being dictated by her alcoholic husband. And my life? I questioned myself.

Instead of answer, all I had was silence.

CHAPTER 33

Two months later, I found out about Lakshmi. Rathna, my new cleaning lady told me the entire incident. I couldn't believe it at all. Lakshmi was in jail.

"Amma, Lakshmi killed her husband to save her daughter. He was trying to sell Gouri to a brothel," Rathna said.

"Are you out of your mind? You want to go to the jail to meet that maidservant?" Vishal was furious when I asked for his permission to allow me to meet Lakshmi.

"Yes, I want to go to the jail to meet that maidservant," I replied in the same tone. I had never been to a police station or a jail before. I was not even aware of the procedure to meet inmates.

"Leela, don't be a fool. What will you do even if you meet her?" Vishal said when he saw desperation on my face.

"I haven't thought about it. My mind is not working, I just want to go and see Lakshmi."

"If you don't know why do you want to go then why are you going?"

"Vishal, I want to meet her," I pleaded.

"You are not going anywhere; I am telling you for the last time. Do you understand?" he shouted.

"Vishal, I have to go. Today I am not going to listen to you. Don't try to..."

Before I could complete my sentence, I felt a hard blow on my cheek.

"You deserve this," he barked.

Holding my cheek, I stared at him, my eyes burning with anger.

"And you deserve this!" I shouted, giving him a hard slap. I didn't know where I got the courage from. My hands didn't wobble at all when I raised my hand at my husband for the first time. It just happened. I didn't bother to think about what would happen later; I was fed up of him controlling my life, I was fed up of being beaten every other day. For the first time, I was not scared of the consequences of my act.

Vishal was too shocked to react. He lifted his hand to hit me again. I ducked just in time. This angered him even more. He lunged at me. I grabbed my handbag from the table and zoomed out, slamming the door shut behind me. I didn't bother to look back to see whether he was following me.

"I want to meet Lakshmi," I spoke to the potbellied jailer at the gate.

"Go and sit in the waiting room. Go inside when your number is called," the jailer said, pointing to a door nearby.

Several people sat on a lone wooden bench in the waiting room. The room was crowded. People elbowed each other to secure a place to stand. Two women with infants sat cross-legged on the floor, in between the legs of people sitting on the bench. They bounced the infants in their laps as they chatted nonstop.

I looked around. The windows were dusty. The walls were shabby with damp spots. The floor was mucky, as if never swept. The stink of sweat and urine was all over. I was the odd one out amongst the relatives of the criminals and accused. After an hour of waiting, the jailer came and blew his whistle. The people in waiting ran towards the other room, like creatures out from a cage.

I followed the crowd. A thin mesh of iron divided the inmates from the visitors. The eyes of inmates searched for familiar faces. People literally climbed over each other to get a glimpse of their near and dear ones.

Lakshmi was elated to see me. "Amma, how are you? How is Anna?" Lakshmi asked giving me a forced smile. She looked pale, but composed.

"Lakshmi, I am sorry. I wish I could've helped you that day." I had been longing to say these words.

"No Amma, it's not your fault. It's my destiny; you have done a lot for me." Her words sounded genuine. "I don't regret anything; my husband deserved this fate."

The room was very noisy. Lakshmi had to shout to make herself heard.

I wanted to comfort her by holding her hand, but the iron mesh between us did not allow it.

"Gouri is in the juvenile home, Amma, girls are not safe there. I am not worried about how many years I will be in jail. I am worried about my daughter. What did she do to deserve this? She wanted to go to school, study and help me, but now..." her voice trailed away, her tears wetting the mesh between us.

"Lakshmi, don't cry, I will do something." My voice was full of promise. "I swear, I will." I was surprised at my own confidence, unaware that the potbellied jailer had blown the whistle indicating the end of visiting hours.

Chapter 34

Vishal's angry face appeared before my eyes when I sat in the auto for the journey back home. I touched my cheek; it felt red with humiliation.

A big black lock on the door welcomed me when I reached home. My face fell. Vishal had put a padlock along with the automatic lock. I dusted the stairs with my dupatta and sat there. Darkness had set in. It had started drizzling. A few drops of rain fell on my feet. I shifted one step up, another step and then another. I had nothing to do to pass my time. I took out my mobile and started deleting the old messages. Done. I browsed through the contact list. I paused at Jai's number. I looked at my watch; it was nine p.m. What time was it in New York? What would he be doing this time? Working his charm over the blondes there? Did he know that someone in Bangalore was crazy about him? Did he ever think of me? May be, may be not. Most likely not!

I tried Vishal's number once again. Still switched off; where had he gone? I couldn't go to Sapna's house. She would definitely spread the news and within seconds, the whole building would know that my husband had locked me out of the house. I couldn't go to Harleen's either. She knew of my middle class status but not of my abusive husband.

Priya was my only option.

"How could you tolerate such a scoundrel for so many years?" Priya asked gritting her teeth in anger. "So much has happened to you, and now you are telling me all this?"

I stayed at Priya's place for the next two days but I didn't belong there. I had all the comforts but I was lonely. There was no point informing my parents about it. They would've scolded me for disobeying my husband.

What if he has left me! What if he has committed suicide! I was scared.

After three days, Ma called me.

"Look, Leela! Vishal has asked me not to tell you this, but you are still my daughter-in-law."

I didn't fail to miss the word 'still'.

"He left for Bangkok on a business trip and will return after two months," she said.

I was speechless. How could she be so cold? I understand her son was unstable but an educated woman like Ma! My definition for word educated had started to wobble.

It was past nine p.m. when I reached Patiala. My last meal was on the flight to Delhi- two rice idlis with coconut chutney and a small bowl of fruit. I had washed it down with a cup of black sugarless tea. My parents would never listen to anything against their son-in-law. In their eyes, he was God sent to uplift their daughter.

Mummy rubbed her eyes in disbelief when she saw me standing at the door, my clothes crumpled, my hair dishevelled from the long bus journey from Delhi. Until now, my parents had no whiff of what had happened.

"Where is your luggage?" Mummy asked, looking around me.

Mummy was too choked to utter a word; her motherly instinct had sensed that something was wrong.

It was freezing cold in December. Mummy was wearing the same yellow and green striped hand knitted woollen scarf on her head, which she had been wearing for the past fifteen years. Whenever I visited my parents' house in winters, I saw the same scarf on Mummy. It had become a part of her personality.

"Who is it?" Daddy ji asked from inside.

"Daddy ji, it's me," I said as I hugged Mummy, avoiding looking into her eyes.

Daddy ji rushed towards the door, tightening his shawl around him. "How have you come? By taxi? Where is Vishal? You should have informed us."

"Daddy ji, I have come alone," I whispered, when he looked about frantically, as if his dear son-in-law was playing hide and seek with him.

I came inside and sat on the sofa.

Mummy and Daddy ji followed me, their expressions writ large with curiosity and worry. They sat on either side of me, waiting for me to quell their anxiety. Sanjay and his wife Bindu too gathered around me. I covered my face with my hands and let out the sob that had been stuck in my throat. They let me cry. I cried until I was too tired to cry anymore, then I narrated the incident which led me to Patiala, leaving out the fact that I had hit Vishal.

"Whatever the problem is, you should not have left your house and come. Vishal *jeeju* is very nice, you are exaggerating a bit too much," Sanjay said with a hint of irritation in his voice.

"I didn't leave on my own." I couldn't say anything more.

"She is very tired now. Let her sleep," Mummy intervened. "Bindu, give her one of your salwar kameezes, mine will be too loose for her; she is even thinner than what she was before marriage."

Quickly, the sofa was pushed against the wall, the chairs were stacked on the table to make place for an extra cot in the living room, next to Mummy's. After Sanjay got married, Bindu and Sanjay occupied my old room. Pinky and Sonu, Sanjay's twins, slept with Daddy ji in another bedroom, whereas Mummy slept on the *diwan* in the living room.

After retirement, Daddy ji had started working at a hardware shop. The responsibility of keeping cash and opening and closing the shop was on Daddy ji.

"But Daddy ji, you didn't tell me that the situation was so bad. It is too much at your age to sit in the shop for the whole day. You have already crossed seventy; you didn't have such long working hours even before retirement?"

"But, what else can we do? Sanjay's income is not steady. One month he brings some money, next month again there is nothing. We can't see our grandchildren craving for petty things," Mummy explained when Sanjay and Bindu were not around.

"He is trying… he is trying. He has bad luck, what to do? Whenever he invests in any share, the next day the rate falls, so what can he do?" Daddy ji did not like listening to anything against his son.

I felt as if I was snatching a morsel from the mouth of their grandchildren, but I didn't have a choice. Ma had closed her doors on me. Vishal was too egotistical a man to shift from a stance, once taken. I had rubbed his ego the wrong way, he would never forgive me.

"So what have you decided?" Sanjay was desperate to ask this question. I knew he still hated me.

"What have I decided?" I repeated his question with emphasis on 'I'. "I have never taken any decision in life. In fact, I don't even know how to take a decision; I took just one small decision and look where I have landed."

CHAPTER 35

It was more than a month since I had come to live with my parents. Tongues were already wagging in the neighbourhood. I didn't like to venture out, as I feared that the neighbours would ask me about my husband. Unlike Mummy, I preferred to keep quiet, rather than cook up stories about my life.

"Her husband has gone to Bangkok, so she decided to stay with us for a few months; she will go back after he returns. They have a big house in Delhi. Her sister-in-law lives in *Amrica*," Mummy repeated the same story when neighbours showed undue curiosity about a married daughter's stay in her parents' house. "Our society has become modern, but still there is no respectable place for a woman who has been abandoned by her husband," Mummy said.

I was startled by the word 'abandoned' used for me. If Mummy had spoken like this before my marriage, I would have brought the roof down for using such demeaning words against women, but now I feared arguing about such sensitive topics.

"In spite of education, in our society a widow has more respect than a divorcee," Mummy said. She was in a mood to give lecture on social norms.

Mummy and Daddy ji decided to go to Delhi to discuss the matter with Ma. They went in the morning and were back the same night.

"Your mother-in-law has a lot of allegations against you, Leela! We want to know what exactly had happened," Mummy asked giving me an accusing look. "She was saying, you misbehaved with Kiran's husband, I don't want to use the word that she used for you. And she was also saying you slapped Vishal. Is this true?"

"You hit Vishal *jeeju*?" Sanjay's stare made me feel like a culprit.

"He has been hitting me every day, what about that?" I roared, trying hard to control my tears. "He had been thrashing me brutally all these years, no one intervened, but when I dared to raise my hand just once, everyone is accusing me. And how disgusting of them to point fingers at me! I misbehaved with Kiran's husband? I? Mummy, you know what happened, I told you what he did to me." My voice choked. I didn't want to cry in front of my parents. "How could you people tolerate all this nonsense and sit in front of them?" I shouted at my mother.

"Leela, now the matter is not as simple as you were explaining. Pandit ji was saying that your mother-in-law has contacted him to find a girl for Vishal," Daddy ji said in a low voice as he got up to change.

I looked at my father unable to comprehend what he had just said. Vishal hit me every day, and I kept quiet. When I hit him once, he wanted to divorce me. It appeared that Vishal had used this opportunity to throw me out of his life. It was not that I wanted to go back to that hell, but for how long could I stay in my parents' house? Bindu leaned against the kitchen door and listened to the heated conversation. She remained quiet. She didn't consider it appropriate to interfere.

"Now what?" Sanjay sounded irritated. "Daddy ji, I can't take care of one more person."

"As if you are the one taking care of this family!" Mummy gave him a look. This was the first time I had heard Mummy speaking against Sanjay.

The severity of the situation was dawning on me. There was nothing more complex in life than the situation of uncertainty. What did Vishal want? Divorce, or was he just trying to teach me a lesson? Though I maintained a stoic expression in front of my parents, the thoughts of a lonely life ahead were beginning to haunt me. I was alone even with Vishal but I was always hopeful that one day things would be fine between us.

After winter came spring, and after spring came summer; it was exactly six months since I had descended on Patiala on a freezing cold night. Vishal had not called me even once since I left Bangalore.

Every morning when I got up, I prayed that I would not have a show down with my brother. I prayed for the long life of my parents; I knew that Sanjay was tolerating me only because of our parents. After all, they had some responsibility towards me. After they were no more, he would not take a day to throw me out of the house. I felt guilty for praying for my parents' long life because I needed a roof over my head.

Jai had completely disappeared from my life. His text messages, his husky voice, the twinkle in his eyes, the way he tossed back his head… it seemed like a dream, which happened only in my imagination. His was like a guest appearance in my life. He had triggered a spark in me and left me alone to deal with it. Thinking of the moments when his warm hug on the pavement had kindled feelings of first love brought a flush to my cheeks. Jai had cast a spell on me, which was impossible to wipe out. He was like a pleasant early morning dream. When you wake up, for a few seconds you feel it to be a reality, but as the rays of the sun penetrate into the room and force open your sleepy eyes, the dream fades away, bringing you back to the real world. Jai vanished from my life as abruptly as he had come.

Gradually memories of Jai started becoming hazy in my mind. I feared I might not be able to recognize him if I happened to see him somewhere, though the possibility of a chance meeting with him was almost nil, he in New York, and I in Patiala. "He west, I east; East is east, and West is west, and never the twain shall meet." I was reminded of a line by Rudyard Kipling I had read recently.

I often went to Pushpa di's house to check my emails. My parents didn't have a computer at home. I logged in; though I hardly received any email from anybody but what if Jai had sent me an email! I was disappointed, there was nothing from Jai, but there was an email from a training institute in Bangalore that provided training to RJs aspirants. The next batch of training was to begin after two months. I had almost forgotten that I had gone to that institute in Bangalore to inquire about the courses they offered. They had noted my email ID and promised to revert with the details. The institute didn't guarantee jobs but in the past years, many of their students had been placed as RJs and TV announcers.

It was an excellent opportunity; I would have grabbed it if I were living in Bangalore. Staying in Bangalore was not so much a worry; Priya or Harleen would have obliged but who would bear the expenditure of forty thousand rupees towards the fee. I couldn't be that shameless to ask my friends for the money; they were already doing so much for me. I felt bad for letting go of the opportunity but that was life.

I had nothing to do the entire day except sulk. The feeling of being dependent on my retired father and living a worthless life scraped me from inside. I sometimes went over to Pushpa di's house for chitchat. Unlike my parents, she advised me to break free from my troubled marriage.

It was easier for her to preach because she had a loving family of her own. No one could understand the feelings of a woman to whom no one loved.

Priya and Harleen called occasionally to know about my well-being. Harleen had sent me twenty thousand rupees through someone. She was aware of my parents' economic condition. It was nice of her to offer me financial help but I had some self-respect; I refused to accept the money. I had taken enough from her to enjoy the transitory pleasures of life.

CHAPTER 36

Pushpa di recommended me to a children's library. Nestled amongst the tall Eucalyptus trees on three sides, 'Happy Home' was situated on a small hillock. A majestic neem tree stood guard at the entrance, its twigs bending under its own weight. A green bed of neem leaves had carpeted the narrow road outside, emitting musky scent into the atmosphere. Five cosy interconnected rooms, surrounded by sprawling lush green lawn, made it look like the perfect place to unwind. It was hard to believe that such a place existed in Patiala. Beside a variety of books for children, there was a computer room to browse and play games. The owner of the library was a middle-aged woman who was in look out for a person who could handle everything in her absence including issuing the books, reading stories to children and attending to registration inquiries.

I was in a desperate need for a breather and I fit in the job description perfectly. The morning hours were usually dull as the children were at school and would start trickling in after four. The owner would come only by five and that too for just an hour. I loved reading stories to the bunch of children who thronged the library in the evening. I preferred to call myself a storyteller rather than a caretaker.

At the end of the month, I got my first salary- two thousand rupees. I ran my fingers over the bright shiny notes. I was so very happy. Its value was more than two thousand for me. It was my hard-earned money. My money. It meant the world to me. I bought a box of *ladoos* on my way back home. I was so excited; I called Priya. I didn't want to tell Harleen, even her maid servants earned more than me.

"Priya, I can plan my future now. I want to adopt a child and live independently like you," I said dreamily.

"Leela! Come out of your dream world. How can you be so naive! You can adopt a child only if you are financially sound to take the responsibility of a child. How much do you earn, only two thousand rupees. And you are not even living with your husband."

I didn't let Priya's words kill my desire to live a complete life. Happy Home had given me a flicker of hope. I knew I would find a way out, but how?

CHAPTER 37

Day by day, it was becoming difficult for me to stay at my parents' house. Mummy and Daddy ji were pressurizing me to go back to Vishal. How could I? Vishal hadn't called me even once. Advice, reprimands, emotional blackmail, my parents tried everything. Sanjay's words were always laced with sarcasm. Bindu was not as friendly as she used to be earlier. There were often verbal feuds between Mummy and Bindu, and invariably it was about something what I had said or done.

"Mummy, you always take Leela's side, even if it is her fault," Bindu complained. "You have to, after all she is your daughter and I am your daughter-in-law."

That day, when I reached home, no one was at home except Bindu. After freshening up, I went to the kitchen to make myself a cup of tea. I didn't want to trouble her.

"Bindu! Is there anything to eat? I am starving," I called my sister-in-law when I didn't find anything to eat in the kitchen.

Bindu was in her room. She deliberately kept quiet. From outside, I could see her sitting cross-legged on the bed and knitting a sweater.

"Bindu!" I called again.

"Haven't you cooked dinner yet? I am very hungry." Thumping my feet on the floor, I went to her room. I had to assay a lot of self-control to prevent myself from flaring up.

"Oh, we all had gone for a *kirtan* in the evening and we ate something there so no one is really hungry, but I can quickly make something for you," Bindu replied without making an effort to get up.

"No need."

I went back to the kitchen. I leaned against the window with the teacup in my hand and looked outside. It was dark everywhere. In spite of meagre resources, my parents' life was peaceful before I came to live with them. I didn't want to be a small spark of fire in their contented life.

My life had always been navigated by others. When did I ever have control over my life? I was now angry at myself. I had lived in a dream world all my life, always blaming the circumstances for my own weaknesses. I could never gather courage to stand up to the circumstances. For how long would I keep blaming others for my own shortcomings? And for how long would I keep dreaming - my dreams never aligned with the real world; my dreams and real life never converged at any point. The sound of my sobs every night, when Vishal hit me, still echoed in my mind. It was clear that Sanjay and Bindu didn't want me to live here. Where should I go? What should I do? I found myself at crossroads in life, and unfortunately, all the roads led to dead ends.

CHAPTER 38

When I reached Happy Home in the morning, I found that the building was being painted. The entire place smelled like rotten garbage.

"You can sit in the veranda until the rooms are painted," the painter informed.

I had one book with me to read, but I couldn't sit there; the smell of paint was giving me a headache, my eyes had started burning.

I got up to leave. The blistering wind slapped my face as I walked back home. It was exceptionally hot that day. I looked forward to my rare time alone in the cool confines of my home. No one was at home. Everyone had gone to a neighbouring village to attend the wedding of a distant cousin. I now hated going for family functions. The relatives showed undue curiosity about my marital status.

On reaching home, I slipped my sweaty feet out from the *jutti,* threw my handbag on the sofa and dashed to the bathroom. I could still feel the smell of paint in my nostrils. I brushed my teeth and exhaled a deep breath. I took off my clothes and stood under the shower. The cold water was soothing. I heard the doorbell chime when I was halfway through with scrubbing my body. I frowned at the thought of someone coming to steal my few hours of privacy. I quickly rinsed off the soap and looked for a towel; there was none. As usual, I had forgotten to take it. I hurriedly wiped myself with a hand towel and put on my clothes. The doorbell buzzed again when I was tying the string of my salwar.

I ran barefoot to answer the doorbell, my feet leaving a wet trail on the floor like the pugmarks of a tiger.

There was a soft knock on the door again.

I quickened my steps.

I opened the door. I froze in my place. I stood there with my mouth open. My feet turned to ice - cold against the heat-spewing cement flooring. My face still damp, my clothes almost wet, the droplets of water were trickling from my hair and falling on my kameez. My heart somersaulted in my chest and made thumping sounds like hammer hitting metal. Was I dreaming?

"Surprise!" Jai said, flashing his dimpled smile.

It was not a dream. I was awake... wide awake. Jai often came in my dreams, but I was never able to see his face. Once, in my dream, I was waiting for him at the bus stop. After waiting for him the entire day in the scorching heat, someone informed me that he would reach by the last bus for the day. I brightened in anticipation, but when the bus came, there was no one inside.

Another time I dreamt that I was waiting for him outside a cinema theatre, but when he didn't turn up, I started walking towards his house. Though I didn't know the address, I located his house somehow. I rang the bell and waited for him to answer. No one opened the door.

It always happened, just when I was about to meet him, someone would wake me up, ending the dream.

"It is because he can never be yours, your dreams are warning you not to chase a mirage," Pushpa di gave her own interpretation when I confided in her about Jai.

But today I was sure Jai was not a mirage. For a moment, I forgot where I was; everything looked surreal. The only thing real was Jai – he was standing just three feet away from me in flesh and blood, at my door. S.J. Venkataraman, my heartthrob was in front of me, just to see me. My heart did a somersault once again.

I gestured him to come in without uttering a word. I was glad I had had the time to take a bath. Imagine meeting him with muck and grime on my face.

I noticed the air of New York had done wonders to his complexion. He looked like a college boy in a white T-shirt and blue denim jeans. He had gained weight slightly, which only enhanced his boyish charm making him look more charming.

His tight fitting T-shirt accentuated his broad shoulders and toned arms. His hair had grown, a little longer than what he used to sport earlier. "I had some work in Patiala. Since I am here, I thought of coming over to see you," Jai said as he lowered himself on the sofa in the living room.

How did he come to know that I was in Patiala?

"I ran into your friend Priya at an official function where she was a special invitee," he explained. "Since you had told me about her, I went up to her and asked about you."

How was he always able to read my thoughts?

I sat on the other end of the sofa, my body twisted towards him. I didn't make an effort to move my hand when the tips of our fingers touched. His touch was electrifying. I still couldn't believe that he was sitting within hugging distance. My heart was thumping loudly. I was sure he could hear my heartbeat. I unsuccessfully tried to conceal my excitement, but the glow on my face must have revealed all. I was blushing from ear to ear. Anyway, I always did a lousy job at hiding my feelings.

"I am so sorry to know about you. Priya told me everything." He took both my hands in his. "You should have called me at least. You had my number."

"Call and do what?"

"I am sorry, extremely sorry," he said tightening his grip on my hands. "Now leave everything and come with me. I am now the resident editor of New Times in Bangalore. I can help you in getting some job in our office," Jai said.

I looked at him, unable to grasp what he was saying.

"Not sure, if I want to shift back to Bangalore. I will think about it," I said slowly.

"But why don't you want to come with me?" he asked.

I smiled, my smile reaching my eyes. He smiled too. The smile turned into laughter. I was so pleased with myself. I was not able to handle the excitement of meeting him; just the thought that he was in front of me was making me go crazy.

There was so much I wanted to say, but it was as if he understood everything. It was as if he had never gone anywhere. He was there, when my husband beat me mercilessly, when he threw me out of his house, when Navin molested me, when I cried in my pillow every night for being so alone and helpless, when I had to swallow my pride every time Sanjay taunted indicating me to leave his house, and like a shameless person, I continued to stay on. It was as if Jai had always been there with me.

"Okay, I will leave now." He got up suddenly. His habit of abruptly terminating the conversation hadn't gone.

I too got up. He stood in front of me, our bodies merely inches apart. His eyes said what his lips didn't. Looking into my eyes, he moved his hands over the small of my back. I melted into him. He gently brought his face forward and planted his lips on mine. I closed my eyes lightly inhaling his warm breath. I could taste Colgate on his lips. Inadvertently, my hands reached for his shoulders. He wrapped his arms around my waist. We kissed first gently and then fervently. I could feel the frenzy in his kiss. I felt myself responding with equal fury. A rush of electric sensation was rippling through my body. At that moment, nothing else mattered in life; it was just us – Jai and me. The kiss radiated a tingling sensation in my mouth, a sensation I had never experienced before - the sensation of a first kiss.

I could tell that this was not the first time for him. He was an experienced kisser, and a wonderful one.

"Not a day has passed when I haven't thought of you," I blurted out, when he took his lips off mine.

"I know that," he said rubbing my cheek with the back of his hand. He looked into my eyes; my eyes flickering with light and hope. He rested one hand on the wall behind me and with the other hand pushed back strands of hair from my face. He pulled me still closer. I neither stepped back, nor resisted. I longed for him like never before. My sweetheart was no longer a dream.

It was a heady feeling when the man who was the heartthrob of many gorgeous women wanted me. Yes, me, whom no one loved. This was the most beautiful moment of my life. I had waited for the day when Jai would reciprocate my love. Not sure, if it was love, infatuation or he was just sympathetic towards me. I didn't know, and I didn't care. I wanted to drown myself in that momentary bliss.

Jai had come and gone like a sea wave, which slips from the grip when one tries to catch it, leaving the person unsteady; but this wave had not unsteadied me. If I had Jai's love, I could move any mountain. It was worth the wait.

"Missing u," a text from Jai appeared after some time.

"Missing u 2," I pressed the reply button without deliberation.

It was past ten when everyone returned home. I quickly made the beds for them.

Jai was amusing me by forwarding jokes.

"Who is calling you so many times at this hour?" Mummy spoke from her bed.

"Dadi, that is the message tone," Pinky replied.

"It's the same thing," Mummy said, as she got up to increase the speed of the fan.

"Mummy, some crap messages from marketing people." I smiled to myself.

I kept my cell phone under my pillow and closed my eyes. Let me sleep Jai, don't come in my dreams, I said to myself.

Soon I was fast asleep.

"Leela! Your phone is ringing," Mummy called from her bed at midnight.

Not at this hour, Jai, I mumbled. I fumbled for my phone in the dark.

"Hello," I whispered bringing the phone closer to my ears, my eyes still closed tightly.

The next moment, I was sitting upright with my eyes wide open, listening in utter disbelief to the voice on the other end.

CHAPTER 39

"Room Number 7, the second room to the right," the attendant at the nurses' station directed me to the private ward.

I stood in the doorway. Vishal lay on the bed with his eyes closed. He looked so calm. A glucose bottle hanging from the mounted stand was connected to his arm through a tube. A bandage was wrapped around his left wrist. Ma sat by his bedside, her face half covered by the newspaper she was reading. There was that same signature expression on her face - nonchalant and determined towards some imaginary goal. I was seeing my husband after one year. Husband... I pondered over the word and my soul laughed a little. The meaning of husband had been quite different for me.

I was devoid of any emotions towards him as if he was just anyone. I threw a glance at Ma. What was the need to inform me now? Let him die or live! Did he bother to call me even once to find out about me, I thought. I hadn't come to Delhi out of any concern for him. My parents insisted that I must go to see him.

I observed Vishal; he had lost weight and looked older than his thirty-nine years. His hair had turned grey at the temples. His eyes were sunk into their sockets and cheeks appeared hollow.

I remembered the last time I saw him, his face red with anger when I was hell bent on meeting Lakshmi in jail, the day I had raised my hand at him. That day felt like it was from another era.

"Leela, thank God you have come!" Ma got up from her chair when she saw me standing in the doorway.

"Ma, how is he now?" I went up to Ma and touched her feet.

She gave me a cold hug. I could sense it. It was so mechanical.

"Leela beta, look what Vishal has done! If you were with him, you would've prevented him like you always did," Ma said, trying to make an extra effort to sound emotional.

Get lost! I wanted to shout.

"He couldn't live with the guilt that he had locked you out of the house. He was too ashamed to even call you," Ma said. "Leela, you don't know how much he cried after he regained consciousness this morning."

Then she narrated in detail how Vishal slit his wrist. While she spoke to me in a low voice, she threw a glance in his direction now and then to check if he was getting disturbed by her talking.

"He was depressed because you left him," she said, winding up the conversation.

I didn't believe her story. She was a manipulative woman and Vishal was a chauvinist. They were making it up. Ma knew that it was not I who left him, then why was she blaming me.

"Vishal look! Leela has come to meet you." Ma lightly touched Vishal's head. Vishal opened his eyes slowly and looked at his mother. Ma held his forehead and slightly tilted his head towards me. Vishal looked surprised to see me, perhaps he didn't know that

Ma had called me or he didn't expect me to come. My lips parted to give a half smile. To be honest I didn't feel anything. He was my husband but I felt no affection, no sympathy. I moved closer to his bed. Tears welled up in his eyes. Taking my hands in his, he cried like a small child. I took my spot on his left, the rightful place of a wife. I sat next to him at the edge of the bed maintaining a distance.

I didn't know how to console a crying man. And why was he crying, was it because he had survived his suicide attempt once again or because his good-for-nothing wife was not there to stop him and he was actually going to die?

"Don't leave me... don't leave me and go... I can't live without you," He cried, his tears wetting my hand.

"Don't cry Vishal, Leela has come back now; she will take care of you," Ma said, stroking his hair.

I looked at Ma. An ungrateful and selfish woman! But she was a mother after all. I wasn't sure if I could blame her.

Vishal was discharged in the evening. I wondered if I was informed about his suicide attempt to nurse him to good health. But, Ma took charge of her son. She fed him, gave him his medicines on time, read newspaper to him, and even stayed awake at night when he complained of uneasiness in his stomach. I was asked to stay by his side to ensure that he didn't attempt suicide again. Anyway, since I was there, I decided to stay on until Vishal was up on his feet. It was odd to sleep by the side of my husband in our old bedroom upstairs. I noticed that he was careful enough to maintain a physical distance from me though the warmth in his voice was conspicuous when he spoke to me. He asked me about my life in Patiala which I answered in monosyllables. I felt he genuinely wanted to know what I did in the past one year. For years, I craved for his affection and finally when he was making attempts for the same, I had ceased caring for him. I chuckled at my fate.

We remained quiet most of the time except indulging in small talk when the silence between us would become unbearable.

"I have been promoted as the Regional Marketing Head of my company," Vishal told me proudly, one day. Then he gave me a snippet of his professional accomplishments in the last one year. He had shuttled between Bangkok, Delhi and Bangalore for most part of the year.

"Our sales office in Bangkok is now fully functional. I am not required there permanently though I will have to make frequent trips to Bangkok. I will be based in Bangalore," he said.

After a week, when Vishal had almost recovered, I informed Ma that I wanted to return to Patiala.

"After you left him, this was the second time he attempted suicide; the Bangalore weather is bad for my asthma else I would've gone to stay with him, and he can't leave his job. There is no one to look after him in Bangalore. What if he tries to commit suicide again!" Ma said. "Leela, Please come back home. I have advised him, he will not raise his hand at you again."

"Ma, it was not my decision to leave him. And now, after a year of staying separately, I can't take this decision with the snap of a finger. I need to think."

Gladly, she didn't persist. Going back to Vishal was a big No. Even if he never raises his hand again, what about the wounds he gave to my soul? What about the insults he showered me with?

What about the humiliation when his brother–in-law molested me and he blamed me?

It was different that I was not welcome in my parents' house too. I knew I would have to find an alternative soon, but I couldn't afford to live independently. At that moment, I had no choice but to return to Patiala.

The next day when I was packing my luggage, Vishal came to the room. He had gone to the bank with Ma.

"Why are you packing your luggage now, we are leaving after three days?" Vishal asked.

"I am going back to Patiala," I said without looking up from the suitcase.

"Leela, please don't go. I want you to come along with me to Bangalore," he said in a pleading tone.

I was not surprised. I was used to his habit of apologizing after every evil act he committed.

"I have to go, I have my job there," I replied, my face bent over my suitcase. I expected him to make fun of my children library job, which gave me a pittance, but he didn't.

"Let me do it," he offered, when he noticed that I was unable to close the suitcase. "Look, how untidily you have dumped your clothes in this. How will it close?" He started taking out clothes from the topmost layer and folding them neatly.

"I can do it myself; I am used to doing my own things," I replied, without looking at him. I dreaded that I might melt under the onslaught of his emotional pleading. I didn't want to get trapped into the same web of lies.

"Leela, you will get plenty of jobs in Bangalore; I will help you find one," he said throwing his arms around me. "I know I am not worth your forgiveness, but please give me another chance. I am a changed person now," he beseeched, bending over to touch my feet.

I pulled away. "Vishal, don't demean yourself like this."

"May be we would've been together if we had a child of our own," he said as if talking to himself.

"Leela, I forgot to tell you. I went to meet Lakshmi in jail when I had visited Bangalore last month. She was saying that she wanted to put Gouri for adoption," he said.

I gave him a surprised look.

He spoke after a long pause.

"Do you want to adopt Gouri? I am sure you long for a child like any other woman," he proposed. "May be this way, you will feel less guilty for what happened with Lakshmi."

I stopped what I was doing. He was always against adoption. I still remember his rude voice when he shooed away Lakshmi that night. But the tone in his voice now, it said that he was not lying.

At night, I tossed and turned in bed. I got down from the bed and looked outside the window, as if it would solve my dilemma. It was dark. The darkness of the night was punctuated by barking of stray dogs on the street. Something made me believe that Vishal meant every word of what he said. Probably, he had realized my worth after staying separately from me for a year.

"Leela, you can adopt a child only if you are financially sound to take the responsibility of a child. How much do you earn, only two thousand rupees. And you are not even living with your husband." Priya's words echoed in my mind.

I hadn't yet replied to the email from the RJ training institute; the option was still open.

Call it a compromise, adjustment, or selfishness; I agreed to return to my marital home. I had no emotional attachment with Vishal. Too much had happened between us to wipe everything and start our life from a clean slate. Marital bliss was no longer my priority. I told myself again that I was moving in with Vishal because I wanted to adopt a child and take up the training for RJ, which was possible, only if I went back to Bangalore. He had agreed to pay the fee. Vishal too wanted me for a purpose; I knew he didn't love me. But I was sure of one thing, if Vishal ever raised his hand at me again, I would not only report it to the police but leave him at that very moment.

I would not be a silent sufferer. I wouldn't allow him to torture me anymore! I said in my mind, with gritted teeth.

CHAPTER 40

It had been six months since I returned to Bangalore. Vishal and I had made a genuine effort to bring normalcy back to our lives, Vishal by controlling his anger, and I, by erasing all painful memories from my mind. I wanted to give my marriage another chance. On my insistence, Vishal had agreed to shift to another apartment complex. I wanted to let go of the past and start my life afresh. That was the only way to move forward.

Vishal spoke very little, even lesser than before. I was not sure whether it was a deliberate attempt by him to avoid any confrontations between us, or whether he had really become more withdrawn. It seemed to me that like me, he too wanted to make a genuine effort to make peace.

Harleen was ecstatic when I met her. "I am soooo... happy for you, Leela!" she said, as she hugged me. "Nothing like your own home and it is an excellent decision to adopt a girl child."

Priya was agitated when I called her. "You shouldn't have come back to your husband. Remember, men never change," she gave me an earful on the phone. "And how are you going to ensure the well-being of your child if your husband starts hitting you again? You should have watched him for some more time before taking the responsibility of another human being."

I laughed. What would she know about men? She was neither married nor had she ever been in a relationship.

"Priya! You have to be in a relationship with a man to understand him," I wanted to say.

Both the men in my life were changed persons. I smiled to myself.

I had called Jai three months ago.

"It's your choice Leela, you know the best," he had said plainly, when I informed him about my patch-up with Vishal.

There was no urge in me to have a romantic relationship with Jai. Moreover, from his side too, it appeared that it was merely a feeling of sympathy, which attracted him to me. It was enough for me to just talk to him over the phone occasionally. I didn't accept his offer of joining New Times. I was scared that our physical proximity might ignite my subdued emotions for him. I sincerely wanted to move on this time. Jai was always my dream and would remain so. I forced my heart to believe that it had been infatuation, and not love, all along, and whatever happened between us in Patiala was just momentary, where both of us succumbed to physical attraction.

For Jai, I was one amongst his many female friends, but not a special friend. Meesha was his fiancée – a girl his parents had chosen for him. Jai going for an arranged match - I was surprised. He had emailed me her photograph. She was a stunning woman and an intellectual like him. They looked like a made for each other couple. Jai was no longer an influencing factor in my life. Vishal or Jai, I didn't want anyone. My priorities in life were stark clear-become an RJ, adopt Gouri and finish my graduation through Open University. There was nothing else on my mind. I wanted to realize my dreams. Love could wait, life couldn't.

Vishal had become indifferent to whatever I did. He would nod to whatever I said. There was no warmth in our relationship. It was like we both needed each other for a purpose – he was abiding by his mother's diktat, and I needed him to adopt a child and pay my fee for the RJ training. As long as he didn't abuse me mentally or physically, I was fine with the arrangement.

Vishal and I went to meet Lakshmi in jail to seek her consent about adoption.

"I must have done some good in my previous life. That's why Gouri is going to become a part of your family. Now I can die in peace!" Lakshmi was ecstatic when she heard what we had to say.

Priya's efforts and high connections cut short the procedural delays for adoption. The formalities were almost complete. In a fortnight, we were to bring Gouri home. Everything was happening at such breakneck speed giving me no time to digest that I would soon be a mother.

She would call me Mummy. Magical! Just Magical! My ears craved for that one word but I had apprehensions. Would I be a good mother to a six-year-old child? I didn't want to daydream. I wanted to savour the moments as they came.

For the first time in my life, everything was happening as per the plan. I was a contented person. But the best part of my life was yet to come. My training was almost complete. Becoming an RJ was not as glamorous as it appeared to be. There was a lot of hard work but I was enjoying every moment of my journey towards my dream. I had learnt to speak functional Kannada, of course with a

Punjabi accent. After English, I was going to speak Kannada with a Punjabi accent. No big deal.

There were a few openings in the local radio stations. I had applied everywhere. I had received a call for the audition from one of the radio stations. Out of thirty-nine applicants, only three students including me had cleared the first round of interview. I was confident of clearing the final audition. I was inching closer to my dream.

There was too much excitement around me. Next day, we had to go to the adoption centre to bring Gouri home. She would legally be our daughter. Vishal didn't appear to be excited about it, but I didn't care much. I had zero expectations from him. As long as he was not putting roadblocks in the way of my happiness, I had no issues. He had produced evidence that we were happily married and he had a steady source of income to take the responsibility of a child. I could adopt a child only because of him; he was of some use to me at last.

Coincidently, I had my final audition on that day.

"Good Morning Bangalore, this is RJ Leela... not just Leela but RJ Leela..." I stood in front of the mirror and practised in my singsong voice.

There was no way I could miss it. This was my dream. I had waited so long for it, but I had to also personally go to the adoption centre and bring Gouri home.

I called Priya to inform her about my dilemma.

"Don't worry; let Gouri come with me straight from the adoption centre. In fact, let her stay with me for a few days. Hansa also has holidays these days. The girls will enjoy together," Priya suggested.

I heaved a sigh of relief. Priya had a solution to all my problems. I thought it was better to inform Vishal about it before hand, as he didn't approve of my friendship with Priya though it was different that I didn't care much for what he liked or disliked. Even before I could complete my sentence, he nodded and went out to wait for me in the car. It appeared that he was upset over something. Anyway, I didn't bother.

Priya and Hansa greeted us with a bouquet of red roses when we reached the adoption centre.

"May your life always blossom and spread happiness around like these roses," Priya said as she hugged me. She greeted Vishal with a cold hello. She showed me a pink frock and a pair of matching shoes that she had brought for Gouri. How thoughtful of her!

I had visited the centre many times earlier; Vishal had accompanied me once to fill up the forms. Priya had completed all formalities before we reached. She had made things smooth for us. We had to only sign on the legal documents and take the child home. I was not enveloped with motherly feelings as I was supposed to be, the way I had read in novels or seen in movies. Was it normal? Shouldn't I be over the moon and shedding tears of joy because I was becoming a mother? Frankly, I didn't feel anything at all. Was it because Gouri was not my biological child? Perhaps, things were happening at too fast a pace to sink in. I wanted to feel excited but I wasn't. May be, I would feel like a mother when Gouri would start living with me. Gouri was an affectionate child and I knew she would fill our lives with love.

We were a family – I, Vishal and our adorable daughter Gouri- a happy family, though not an ideal one.

"Bye - Bye Gouri, I will come on Sunday to take you home." I waved to my dear daughter as she sat with Hansa in the backseat of the car while Priya was at the wheel.

CHAPTER 41

My final audition for the job of RJ went off very well. I had to be a mock RJ to demonstrate if I was spontaneous and could engage listeners. The station director was very impressed with me.

"Hey Leela! You speak like an experienced RJ," the station director complimented me when I was leaving.

"Thanks, it has always been my dream." I glowed with happiness.

I was confident I would get the job.

If selected, I would have to host a four-hour breakfast show every day. For four hours, I would have to speak almost nonstop, what would I speak on? Would I have sufficient content to speak? Of course, I would have my team to assist me but I would have to keep myself updated with all the latest in music, films, current affairs and everything else. It would be really challenging but it was going to be fun. I was sure, I could do it. I had it in me. I knew I was born to be an RJ. True, when your time is good, only good things happen with you.

I still couldn't believe that I was so close to my dream. I sat in the bus to go back home.

I was so excited, I desperately wanted to share this moment of happiness with Jai, I had spoken so much about becoming an RJ in my chats with him on Facebook, and now when I had almost accomplished my mission, he wasn't there in my life. I picked up the phone to call him but then decided against it.

When I reached home, Vishal was already there. He generally returned much after me.

"So early today?" I asked.

"Early? It is nine o'clock," he said pointing towards the watch on his wrist.

"Oh, you know the traffic at this hour." I smiled.

I expected him to ask me about my interview but he didn't.

I saw three open bottles of liquor and a glass on the table. Vishal drank rarely, and when he did, it was in moderation. It looked that he had been drinking for a while.

I sensed something was wrong. He seemed to be in a foul mood. He looked so angry, I thought he was about to slap me. I preferred to keep quiet; I didn't want to poke a beehive. He was still very unpredictable. I threw an uneasy glance at Vishal before darting to the kitchen to prepare the dinner.

"Who is S.J.Venkataraman?" he asked, following me to the kitchen.

I was taken aback on hearing Jai's name. My smile faded. How did Vishal know Jai? I hadn't met Jai since I returned to Bangalore though I had spoken to him a few times.

I looked back.

"Why, what happened?" I asked, concealing my nervousness. I could feel my face turning white. I dared not tell Vishal about Jai. Though Jai was just a friend, a husband, however modern he was, could never tolerate his wife's male friends. And Vishal was very conservative in thoughts; I was sure he would never accept the fact that I was good friends with another man.

"Don't ask 'why'; tell me who this bloody guy is!" Vishal shouted flaring his nostrils.

Before I could decide how to deal with this situation, he shoved some papers at my face and growled. "So that's what kept you busy today? And every day?"

I looked at the papers. They were the itemized bills of my cell phone for the last eight months, with Jai's phone numbers encircled in red. He had also sourced the earlier bills, when I used to talk to Jai even more often. The bills were testimony to my growing association with Jai.

"I had to spend sixty thousand rupees to be able to listen to you talk with your lover," he snarled.

I couldn't believe Vishal had become so suspicious of my fidelity that he'd spend such a large amount on getting the recordings of my calls with Jai.

"For how long has this been going on?" he asked sternly, lighting a cigarette.

I could no longer hold my cool. So he had been spying on me. He had the cheek to not only procure my itemized bills, but the recordings of my phone calls with Jai.

"How long has what been going on?" I spat.

"Now I understand, why you immediately agreed to come back to Bangalore; I should have sensed this that time itself," he mocked.

"What are you talking about, Vishal?" I shouted; I was not able to control myself.

"You bloody bitch!" He raised his fist to hit me, but he didn't.

I was horrified. A cold shiver passed through me. His body language, his taunts, I could see the old Vishal emerging. I was scared to wits. There was no way I could get away with it all by saying that I didn't know Jai. The evidence was in front of him.

I spilled the beans. I narrated everything, right from day one, when I had met Jai in his office a few years ago for a job. I didn't have the courage to divulge that he had come to meet me in Patiala. Vishal would kill me.

"Vishal! Jai is just a good friend, nothing more; he is getting married next month," I said.

"Oh, so you call him Jai... very romantic!"

Before I could open my mouth again to defend myself, Vishal picked up the liquor glass from the table and hurled it at me. Narrowly missing my right eye, it hit my forehead and smashed to bits when it fell to the ground. Drops of blood appeared on my fingers when I touched the bump on my head.

Vishal smashed one of the liquor bottles against the wall. Then glasses, plates and a vase followed; my drawing room resembled a war zone.

I started trembling with fear.

"Help me!" I shouted.

Vishal kept hurling abuses and throwing things. When he was done and there was nothing else around to throw, he grabbed me by my hair and shoved my face into the sofa, yelling at me all the time for being unfaithful.

I opened my mouth to yell back.

He slapped me across the face.

"You whore!" He pulled me by my hair again, and spit on my face. He slammed me against the floor, cursing violently.

I was angry too. I was hurt and I was dead scared.

My sobbing only served to fuel his rage. He then kicked me in the stomach. He picked his cigarette up from the floor and pressed it against my arm.

I shrieked with pain. The force of his blows in the dead of the night was loud enough to be heard outside the four walls of our apartment.

"Please leave me, leave me..." The more I begged for mercy, the more he kicked. Then he grabbed the back of my neck. I tried to pull back. He squeezed my neck so hard that I was gasping for breath. My head started to roll back. I couldn't take the hitting anymore. God, why didn't he just kill me and get it over with?

"Kill me if you have the courage, you butcher!" I challenged him.

"I will not kill you. I will torture you so much that you will beg for death," he shouted giving me another kick in my stomach. "You bitch! How dare you cheat on me?"

Blood oozed from the corner of my lips. I curled up on the floor, writhing in pain.

In that state, as I felt half-dead, I saw someone standing in their balcony, opposite our apartment. The balcony was at quite a distance; that person must not have heard anything, but I was sure that he or she could see what was going on. I didn't care even if the entire world knew that my husband beat me mercilessly. I had made a big blunder by trusting Vishal again. I wished that he would've died.

Suddenly, Vishal let go of me and sprinted to the balcony.

"I will kill myself. I will die; I don't want to live in this world anymore." I heard him say from the balcony.

I felt a surge of panic, thinking of his previous suicide attempts. I wanted Vishal to really commit suicide this time. I longed for freedom. I prayed for his death!

In that sub conscious state, my eyes barely open, my hair all over my face, I knew that my life would not change as long as the monster was alive.

"What if I push him down?" The sudden thought jarred me. My heart started to thud. What if I just did it? Yes, that would end all my problems. It would.

I pushed myself up on an elbow, but fell down again. I had no energy to get up.

I saw him leaning over the balcony.

My hands started shivering. I tried to get up again, but my body refused to move.

My hands were already quivering. My knees were wobbling, thinking of my evil intention, but I had to decide quickly. Maybe I had made a decision already, but I wasn't able to accept it.

"I will die, and then you can go and live with your Jai." His tone had become soft. He spoke in murmurs; he was probably drained of his energy. I was not sure whether that was because the effect of his drinks had subsided or because he had realized that his threats were hollow.

"Leela! Save me." I heard a voice faintly.

I could now see only his face. Vishal had climbed down the railings and didn't know how to come up. He was stranded there at the edge.

"Save me. I am falling down." I heard his voice again.

I gathered the strength to get up from the floor and limped towards the balcony.

I am going to push him, I decided...

No, I can't kill him; I will divorce him, I will leave this house right now.

No, he won't let me live peacefully, I will kill him.

He is my husband. How can I murder him? The conversation within my head was raging. I didn't know what I wanted to do.

He was standing on the narrow parapet, looking expectantly in my direction.

"Leela, please pull me up. I am fainting," he begged, his eyes full of remorse.

I limped in his direction. I bent down - to reach him or push him down, I still didn't know. Vishal was looking at me with pleading eyes. There were only a few inches of distance between us. I could either give him life, or take it. I felt a surge of power. For the first time in life, the ball was in my court.

Should I?

Shouldn't I?

I stretched out my arm.

"That woman pushed someone down!" I heard the woman in the opposite balcony scream before I passed out.

CHAPTER 42

"Eh, get up! Someone has come to meet you." I heard a gruff voice wake me up.

I opened my eyes and stared blankly at the face above me.

I couldn't keep my eyes open; they were hurting.

"Get up! You have to go." I felt someone shake my shoulder roughly.

I slowly opened my eyes again. A policewoman was looking at me.

I realized I was in the police station.

"That woman pushed someone down." I recalled the words.

I didn't know what happened after I saw Vishal falling down from the parapet. Who informed the Police? How was I brought to the police station? What happened to him after he fell down? Is he really dead? Did I push him? I? Was it so easy? May be he fell before my fingers could touch him. I was confused.

I tried to get up but I couldn't. My whole body ached. It was as if every part of my body was broken. I touched my eyes; they felt swollen. I could barely open them. I made another futile attempt to get up from the floor. When I couldn't, the policewoman bent down on her knees and helped me stand up. Holding me by my arm, she brought me out of the cell I was locked in.

When I came out, I found Priya sitting across from the police inspector. She got up when she saw me. She stepped towards me. Priya didn't say anything, just hugged me tight, something which I needed badly.

"We have to go to the crematorium. Your parents - in- law have already arrived from Delhi," she said, caressing my hair when we fell apart.

I knew Vishal was dead. How could anyone survive the fall from the seventh floor! I thought as I slowly walked along with Priya to the waiting police vehicle outside.

Priya and I were bundled into the back seat of the vehicle along with two policewomen sitting across from us. A male police constable got into the front seat next to the driver.

Priya took out a hairbrush from her bag and combed my dishevelled hair, all the while comforting and consoling me that it would all be fine. I was in too dazed a state to utter a word.

"I tried reaching your friend Harleen. I found her number in your phone. You had told me once that she is very influential. She is in California right now. She said she knows a very good lawyer," Priya said.

I was giving trouble to many people. My life had become a whirlpool of mess. The more I tried to come out of it, the more I was getting sucked into it.

"I haven't informed your parents. Your father is a heart patient. They would unnecessary take the trouble of coming to Bangalore, and what will they do even if they come," Priya said.

I didn't know what would be more shocking to them- Vishal's death or my arrest.

"Gouri?" I parted my lips slowly, turning my neck in her direction.

"Don't worry about her. I haven't told her anything. She will stay with me until everything is fine," Priya said, wiping the dried blood at the corner of my lips with a wet tissue.

The police vehicle stopped outside the crematorium. Priya got down first. She held my hand to help me step down from the vehicle. She guided me to a small hall.

In the centre of the hall, Vishal's body lay wrapped in a white sheet - his favourite colour. There was no outburst of emotions when I saw the dead body of my husband. I had become emotionally numb. I was expected to look devastated at the death of my husband and I appeared devastated because of last night beatings but frankly, I felt nothing.

A handful of mourners, both men and women stood there with hands folded to the dead body. They greeted me in polite namaste when I walked in. They must be from his office, he didn't have any friends, I thought.

Ma was performing *puja* to the dead body. I stood next to her with my hands folded to Vishal's body. She didn't look in my direction. I expected her to comfort me but she didn't.

Does she think that I have killed her son, or she thinks it's a suicide, I wanted to know.

Papa stood on her other side. It was the first time Papa was visiting Bangalore. Except at the time of our marriage and a few other occasions, I had never seen the father and son together.

That day, he had left everything to stand by the side of his son's dead body - nothing came in his way. I performed the ceremonies as instructed by the priest, just the way I had done so at the time of my marriage. I still didn't understand the significance of those useless customs. Ma went about the last rites maintaining a stoic expression. She appeared very much in control of her emotions. After the *puja,* Vishal's body was taken to the furnace room.

I still couldn't believe that I had killed my tormentor. Did I really kill him? One small push and it was over. It was over for him but not for me. I was only twenty-nine and had not seen the world enough. Priya said, life begins at forty but mine was ending at twenty-nine. I was an accused charged with my husband's murder; the reality was slowly dawning on me. What if the charges are proved in the court! What if I meet the same fate as Lakshmi's ! I almost fainted thinking about it.

Ma and Papa returned to Delhi from the crematorium, and I was sent to jail.

It was ironical that I was locked in the same cell as that of Lakshmi's. One day I was consoling her, that day she was consoling me.

There was no ventilation and natural light in the ten by four room that I was locked in. The stench of urine and sweat permeated everywhere. In my cell, there were nine other inmates, who were undergoing trial for murders, dacoity, and human trafficking. I had joined the league of hard-core criminals. Seemed like a page from a fictional story that I was reading.

There was not enough space to even spread legs while sleeping. We slept in shifts. When a few would go to the court during the day, others would use the space to sleep. The hard floor below felt like rock. We were considered fortunate; in our prison, there was no water shortage. We got sufficient for wash and bath, in some prisons I was told, there was no water even for toilets. The mosquitoes, flies, insects, pulses which had more stones than grains, I could manage with everything. Out of all the things in the prison, I missed my lemon tea the most.

It was only destiny that I legally adopted Gouri just a few hours before Vishal's death. He served his purpose before dying. It was also destiny that I was charged with murder just a day after I realized my dream of becoming an RJ.

Most of the inmates kept themselves occupied with one or the other work, but a few just sat there staring at the paan- stained walls. When they got bored, they would pounce at each other like hungry tigresses perhaps to channelize their physical energies. Lakshmi told me, those women who were quiet and kept to themselves were often attacked by other prisoners. Lakshmi always came to my rescue when other prisoners indulged in verbal or physical feuds with me. She was my guardian in prison. I started learning candle making. It was very easy. I was given 30 rupees per day as my labour. I also had to chop vegetables and knead dough as a part of my duties.

"Salma and Babita have been in the jail for the past three years without any trial," Lakshmi said when we had just sat for lunch.

I had no evidence to prove that I was innocent. And I was not even sure if I was really innocent. It was over in a blink. By the time I opened my eyes, Vishal was already falling down. And even if I could produce the evidence, the court cases linger on for years, until then I would have to rot in the jail. My bail application had been rejected twice.

It was sad that Vishal didn't let me live peacefully even after his death.

"Amma, don't worry. It will be fine," Lakshmi said, putting a comforting arm around me when she saw my teary eyes.

Hope is such a wonderful thing. One could undergo any misery in anticipation of a better tomorrow. Every time a calamity befell me, I had risen despite everything, and this time too, I could faintly see the open window somewhere. I would fight, not for myself but for that child whose responsibility I had taken. Gouri gave me the courage to fight.

Next day, Harleen came to meet me; she was accompanied by a young woman wearing stylish clothes. The heady scent of expensive perfume filled the room as the duo entered the visitors' room.

"Leela, this is Renuka Nath, a reputed criminal defense lawyer of Karnataka. She is going to fight your case," Harleen introduced us.

I looked at Harleen with gratitude. If God had given me a cruel husband, God had also given me true friends like Priya and Harleen.

I narrated my entire life story, account by account–fraud, physical abuse, molestation, Vishal's suicide attempts, and the thought of pushing him down... I told all.

Renuka made notes while I spoke about my life gone by.

"Don't say in the court that you wanted to kill your husband; say you were trying to save him," Renuka instructed, after I finished. "And remember, don't say that you don't know if you pushed him or he fell on his own, the way you are saying now," Renuka said.

"Harleen, I am only worried about this statement," she said looking towards Harleen. "Your friend is too simple."

The first hearing was just a month away. I was appearing in the court for the first time. I had seen the courtroom only in the movies. It was exactly the same except there were only a few spectators. The way I looked around nervously, anyone could tell that it was my first time.

Public prosecutors were busy leafing through files of cases while chatting amongst themselves. Finally, the magistrate entered, bowed, and took his seat. I was asked to go into the witness box. The magistrate asked the advocate to confirm my particulars, after which he read out the charges against me.

I answered a volley of questions from the lawyer as briefly as I could.

The case was adjourned until the next hearing, which was after one month. There was no evidence in my defence. That woman from my building was the witness to our fight that fateful night.

Renuka and Harleen came to the prison the next day to gather more facts about the last ten years of my life.

One week before the hearing, Renuka informed me that Ma had agreed to testify in the court about Vishal's suicidal instincts.

Would Ma appear in the witness box to defend me! I couldn't believe it.

Ma had collected reports from the hospital to strengthen her testimony. Harleen later told me that a woman sitting next to her in the court mistook Ma for my mother.

The fast track court cleared my case in exactly eight months, and three hearings. It was nothing less than a miracle in a country where innocents perish in jails for years without trial. The court dismissed the murder charge against me. The tears rolled down my cheeks when the magistrate announced the judgement - they were of course tears of happiness, they were also tears for those like Babita and Salma who didn't have influential friends to fight their case.

Ma was standing outside with Harleen and Priya when I came out of the court. She gave me a half smile when she saw me coming towards her, her eyes moist. Her one gesture had washed off her previous sins. I walked up to her. I didn't bend down to touch her feet, I hugged her instead. She hugged me back.

"I cannot get my son back. If by giving a statement in court, I can save you, I will feel less guilty for all that happened to you," she said, wiping her tears.

Epilogue

After One Year - No more a Daydream

I enter the supermarket on my way home from the Radio Station. Usually I host only the morning show but today the RJ for the noon show was on leave so I had to host both the shows. It is evening and the store is full of people. I pick up my groceries and stand in the queue to pay the bill. At that time, my phone rings. I can see the residence number flashing on the screen.

"Hello Gouri, Mamma will be home in twenty minutes," I say in a childlike voice.

Then I ask my daughter about her school, her friends, the homework and such other things that now I am familiar with.

"Excuse me, aren't you RJ Leela?" I hear a voice behind me.

I look back. A young woman is smiling at me.

"I am a huge fan of your shows," she says even before I can nod. "Your voice is so distinct. Anyone who has heard you on radio can make out. It sounds as if you are smiling when you speak," the woman says.

I give her a humble smile. I still don't know how to receive compliments.

There are many people in the queue. They crane their necks to take a look at me. A few smile, others just look as if I am some alien from another planet.

I quickly pay the bill and leave.

As usual Gouri is waiting outside the door when I reach home. I bend down to hug her. She throws her arms around me and gives me a peck on the cheek before rushing inside to inform my parents about me. My parents now stay with me. Sanjay says the house in Patiala is small for six people. I wonder how the house becomes small when parents become old. Sanjay calls me whenever it's time to pay school fees for his kids. I don't mind paying their fees; after all they are my niece and nephew. Ma had a plot in Delhi. She sold that off and transferred the entire money to my account. She says she holds herself partially responsible for the miseries in my life. Though, I don't think so, I appreciate her for the huge money that she has given me. I have kept a small sum for myself and with the remaining money; I have created a fund to help destitute women who would want to have a choice in their lives, something which I didn't have because of my early marriage and less education. Ma has also willed her house in Rajouri Garden in my name. She often asks me to relocate to Delhi but I will never leave Bangalore. I love Bangalore; the city has given me my identity.

Jai is out of my system. Sometimes I feel there wasn't any such person in my life; he is just one of the fictional characters of the stories that I used to read. I have stopped reading fiction now. When real life is as strange as fiction, who needs stories.

This is the second phase of my life, and I love every moment of it.

I have been invited as the chief guest for a Women's Day program of the Forum for Women Welfare. I was surprised when the Director of the Forum approached me with the invitation. She says I am a role model for the society. I am humbled and honoured. I haven't done anything great in life to deserve this honour. The Director wants women to get inspired by me. I told her, no one can learn from anyone. We all have to fight our own battles.

There are three hundred women in the audience. I can also spot a few men. I don't know why but I am damn nervous when I am about to go on the dais. I have never given a speech in front of so many people in my life. Ma is visiting me these days so I have asked her to accompany me. She knows what I am going to talk about. She is okay with it. Ma is flanked by Hansa and Gouri on either side. My parents are sitting next to them. From their lost expressions, I can make out; they can't believe that their daughter has been invited as a chief guest. It is me after all, the inauspicious *Manglik.*

As usual, my friends Harleen and Priya are also with me.

I can see media people in the front row when I am walking towards the dais. There is a storm brewing in my mind. It'll be the first time I will be talking in public about my personal life. Will I be able to relive those years? My curbed aspirations, my painful marriage, my monstrous husband, my fraud in-laws, my incomplete love, the scars on my body, the scars on my soul, a life of slavery, the struggle in jail despite being innocent... but am I really innocent? I am not sure if I pushed Vishal or not. At times, deep inside my heart, a faint voice tells me I did. I did push him. And the same voice tells me that it's okay even if I did. It assures me that I did the right thing. I did what was to be done. That I deserved to be happy and if I had to become a murderer to achieve the same, so be it.

I begin:

Good evening, Ladies and Gentlemen! It is my privilege to be here amongst you all.

I pause. I look at Ma for her approval. I don't want to embarrass her. She nods. I take a deep breath.

They say you can always see a faint light at the end of the tunnel. All you need to do is follow the light and you will be out of darkness. The corridor, I was walking down didn't have a trace of illumination. I couldn't see the other end. But I kept moving and now, when I have reached the other end, I realize that more than the light, you need the determination to keep moving, keep struggling for your dreams, for your existence, for your survival.

I am a victim of domestic violence and fraud in marriage. I look at Ma. She is looking down. I feel sad for her. She has lost her dear son.

I was tried for the murder of my husband. But I survived it all and here I am, talking to you.

I chuckle for a moment. It feels as if I have been transported to a state of trance. I want to say it all, everything that's buried inside me which chokes me, which suffocates me.

When I was born, I was considered inauspicious by my parents. They married me off and I got a husband who used to beat me every other day. I was a puppet in the hands of others. My dreams, my aspirations, my expectations – each time they surfaced, they were raped and murdered.

The pin-drop silence in the room is conspicuous. I feel my eyes getting moist but I continue.

My husband had suicidal tendencies. He was mentally unstable. But I was charged for his murder. I was in jail for months, rotting there. But you know, I feel it was still better than living with my husband. At least the dusk didn't mean that Vishal would return and beat me again! At least the night didn't mean that I will be burnt with cigarettes again.

I look down, take a deep breath again. I am composed. I don't have any grudges against anyone.

But I think I am very fortunate as I am living my dream now. Not everyone gets that. And no struggle can be survived without support. I couldn't have made it without my friends. Not everyone has great friends like I have.

I can see Harleen and Priya smiling.

If you have such friends, cherish them for life. And this is not just my story. There are so many Leelas around you. And those Leelas, they are suffering, they are suffocating, they are shrieking in infinite silence, waiting for someone to come and free them from the invisible shackles. Listen to their screams, which are lost. Look into their eyes, which tell the stories of torture. Decipher their helplessness. It's you, who have to help them out. It's you who have to give them the courage and confidence so that even when there is no light, they can keep moving and reach the other end of the corridor.

End

GLOSSARY

Besan ke ladoo - A dessert made from gram flour, butter and sugar

Diwan - Cot

Manglik – A fault in horoscope

Burfi - A dessert made from milk and sugar

Puja - Prayer ceremony

Mehandi - Henna

Ghunghat - Veil or a scarf worn by a woman to cover her face

Kundan Choker- Necklace made from highly refined gold

Paranthas - Pancakes made from wheat flour

Sehra - Headdress worn by the bridegroom

Gurdwara - The place of worship for Sikhs

Jingbang - A slang to describe a whole lot

Sardarni – Sikh Woman

Seekh kabab- An appetizer made with lamb meat

Mangalsutra-Sacred necklace worn by married Hindu women

Jutti - A flat shoe with extensive embroidery in colourful threads - common in north India

Paneer Makhani - A rich dish made of cottage cheese and cream

Pakoras - Fritters made out of gram flour and vegetables

Aloo parantha - Pancakes made from potato – a staple diet of Punjab region

Kudi - Girl

Jeeju - Sister's husband

Kirtan - A group recital of hymns in praise of God

Page Three party- A name given in India to high society partying